D1337551

LIBERTY TERRACE

LIBERTY TERRACE

Madeleine D'Arcy

Doire Press

First published in 2021

Doire Press
Aille, Inverin
Co. Galway
www.doirepress.com

Layout: Lisa Frank
Cover design: Tríona Walsh
Cover photo: Madeleine D'Arcy
Map: Andrew Lane
Author photo: Claire O'Rorke

Printed by Clódóirí CL
Casla, Co. na Gaillimhe

ISBN 978-1-907682-86-5

We gratefully acknowledge the support and assistance of The Arts Council of Ireland.

To Andrew and Cass, with love.

And in memory of my father, Michael D'Arcy.

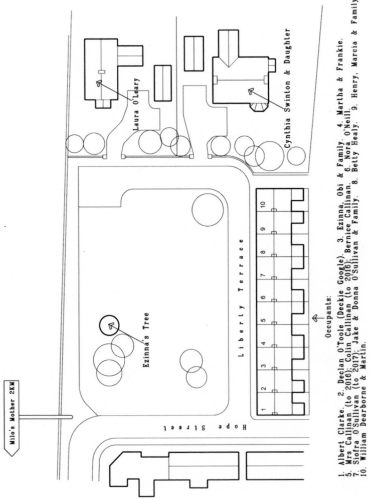

Milo's Mother 2KM

Hope Street

Liberty Terrace

Laura O'Leary

Ezinna's Tree

Cynthia Swinton & Daughter

Occupants:

1. Albert Clarke. 2. Declan O'Toole (Deckie Google). 3. Ezinna, Obi & Family. 4. Martha & Frankie.
5. Mrs Callinan (to 2016); Colin Callinan (to 2016); Bernice Callinan. 6. Nora O'Neill.
7. Siofra O'Sullivan (to 2017); Jake & Donna O'Sullivan & Family. 8. Betty Healy. 9. Henry, Marcia & Family.
10. William Dearborne & Martin.

CONTENTS

TO BE A DEARBORNE

The trouble was I got way too comfortable in the old man's house. Otherwise I'd have never opened the front door.

I'd been lying on the couch in the sitting room with an old tartan rug over me, reading one of the old man's detective books by a fella called Mickey Spillane, and I must have dozed off. When the doorbell rang, I was dreaming I was a small boy running fast to catch up with St Martin De Porres and his little dog... and before I knew what I was doing, I was out in the dusty hallway, unlocking the front door.

It was pelting rain outside and the woman on the door-step looked soaked. She was oldish and wore one of those bright yellow jackets that chuggers wear, over a black raincoat. A heavy-looking black bag hung over her shoulder. Even her glasses were wet.

'Sorry, I have no spare change,' I said and went to pull the door closed as fast as I could.

'Oh, please, hang on. I'm not looking for money. I'm your

Census Enumerator.' She smiled and held up an ID she was wearing around her neck. It looked official, with her photo on it — which freaked me out.

'Senses?' I hadn't a clue what she was on about.

'Everyone in Ireland is being counted on Census Night,' she said. It was next Sunday, 24th April and she'd called heaps of times and posted three calling cards through the letterbox and sure enough they were lying on the hall floor amidst the flyers and takeaway menus. She went on about how the information was used for statistics only and it wouldn't take a minute. I thought I saw a curtain twitch across the street, so I brought her in and shut the door.

'Good to get out of the rain,' she sighed and walked into the sitting room. She sat down on the couch and plonked the bag on the floor beside her. 'To be honest, I'd never have taken this job if I'd known how hard it would be.' She took a tissue out of her pocket and wiped her glasses.

The Mickey Spillane book was on the coffee table, next to the old man's pipe.

'You like crime novels?' she asked.

'Yeah. I've kind of got addicted to them.' That was true. There was no TV, only an ancient wooden box radio. That's why I'd started reading the old lad's detective books, which normally I would never do. I'd tried Sherlock Holmes and some of the Ruth Rendells, but I liked the Mickey Spillane ones best — they were full of action and kind of sexy in an old-fashioned way.

She unzipped the bag and got out an official-looking book. 'This is Number 10 Liberty Terrace, isn't it?'

'Yeah.'

'And what's your name?'

'Martin,' I said. I still wasn't thinking straight.

'Is this your family home?'

'No, it's only me here.'

'Right. All I have to do is ask you a few questions, then I'll come back and collect the form after Census night.'

'Form? I can't fill out no form.'

'Well, it's the law, I'm afraid, but it's easy to fill out.' She looked apologetic.

'See, it's my Granddad's house,' I said, inspired.

'Is your Grandad in?'

'Naw.'

'What's his name?'

'William Dearborne.' Thank fuck I knew it; the old lad had his name written inside the cover of all his books.

She wrote it down. 'Is it just the two of you living here, Martin?'

'Yeah. I keep him company like.'

She ticked a box and looked up at me again.

'Could I have a contact number?'

'Ah, my phone is banjaxed at the moment.'

'Do you have a landline?'

'Oh yeah.' There was an old-fashioned phone in the kitchen. 'I'll get the number.' I called it out to her, but I swapped around the last two numbers.

If there was no one here on Sunday night she said she'd have to fill out a Form E instead, so I said no it was okay and she took out a form and wrote some stuff on it and went on telling me to mark a line for yes rather than a tick and use a black or blue pen and that in a hundred years people could look up their ancestors because of the Census and I said 'What do I care, sure I'll be dead myself then,' but in the end I was saying yeah I'd explain the whole thing to my Grandad and she could come round to collect the form the following Friday and I let her out. Then I locked the front door and went into the kitchen.

After that, I was in bits. The Census woman seemed nice enough, but if she guessed I was squatting, she'd probably put the law on me. She'd be back next week and the thought of sleeping rough again made me feel sick.

See, my stepfather is an abusive fucker. Behind Mam's back he'd always tell me I was a useless thick. After Mam died, he got worse. *Martin, you're named after a black saint. D'you know why? Because your whore of a mother didn't know at the time whether she was having a black baby or a white one.* So, a week ago, I hit him. I'd have had no bother shooting him dead right then, like Mike Hammer in the Mickey Spillane books, only I promised Mam before she died that I'd always try to keep out of trouble. Anyway, I didn't have a gun.

So I ran out the door instead and walked around a while. When I crept in, he was snorting and snoring on the couch as usual, beer cans skittled on the floor. I remembered Mam used to hide cash in the freezer — her 'frozen assets' she used to call it — it was our secret. I found €50 inside her dummy bag of frozen peas, and for a second I thought I'd start bawling. Then I sneaked upstairs, packed a few things and fecked off.

I got the bus to Cork and went straight to the dole office, but I couldn't fill out the form. 'You need a PPS number and your birth cert,' the woman said. When she found out my age, she told me I couldn't get the dole until I was eighteen. Eight whole weeks away. I was gutted.

For a few nights, I slept in the entrance to Penney's — there's a security camera above it, so if someone pisses or pukes on you or beats you up, at least it'll be on film.

Then I was in a squat near the Mercy Hospital, but there

was a fight between some foreign fellas, so the police came and kicked us out. Next day the place was boarded up. A fella told me that if I went to the homeless shelter they'd call up the Child Welfare and put me into a home, so no way was I going to chance going there.

Back out sleeping rough, I was more scared than I was the first time, now I knew what could go down, and all that night I barely slept a wink. The next day, hardly able to keep me eyes open, I was begging in Daunt Square when I had a stroke of luck. Two batty old ladies were chatting about some old fella who'd kicked the bucket above in Liberty Terrace.

'There for three days, God help him.'

'Desperate, wasn't it? Sure, only for the neighbours noticing the lights were on day and night, his body wouldn't have been found for weeks.'

I scoped the terrace out for ages. Number 10 was empty alright. At the end of a terrace with a small alleyway out to the back, no lock on the side gate, it was perfect. I broke the kitchen window and climbed in.

The best thing of all was the old man's kitchen. He had two fridge freezers. One worked and the other didn't. There was only sour milk and old cheese in the fridge part of the one that worked, but there were heaps of ready meals in the freezer part.

I was starving and drenched so I put a curry into the old microwave before I checked out the second fridge. A handwritten sign 'PHARMACY' was sellotaped on it, but all there was inside was bottles of whiskey, cans of coke, a box of mixed biscuits, four packets of Scots Clan, cod liver oil and a packet of paracetamol. When I burst out laughing it sounded strange, because I hadn't laughed in ages.

By the time the Census Lady called, I'd made fearsome inroads on all the food in Number 10. Thank God there was some whiskey and coke left in the PHARMACY, so I poured myself a drink to calm me down. It must have been reading all those detective books that inspired me because after a while I figured I'd try to fill out the form as if the old man was still alive, so I could keep the Census woman off my back for a few weeks. So I went rootling around the house for clues to make it look legit, and found them in a worn brown suitcase on top of the wardrobe in the old man's bedroom.

Take your time, I told myself, like Mam used to tell me. I wrote the form in pencil first so I wouldn't feck it up.

Eleven questions about the house — it wasn't easy to figure out when it was built, but I could handle all the rest.

Person 1: William Dearborne. Date of Birth — no problem, I'd found his birth cert in the suitcase. Widowed, definitely. I had to make up some of the other answers but I kept it simple, though I dithered for ages about the questions on health, since he was actually dead.

Person 2: Martin Dearborne. I was Martin alright, after St Martin De Porres, but I was no Dearborne, and I'd never had a Grandad.

I signed William's name on the form with a shaky black signature. I copied it from the one he wrote in his crime books.

The form looked grand except there was no space to list all the other stuff about William, about the time he'd worked on the oil rigs, about his wife who died so young, and about the little dog Rusty he used to have. I'd already guessed he must have had a dog before I saw the photos, because a red leather collar and lead still hung from a hook in the hall. I liked old William; he wasn't just some sad old fuck. I wouldn't have minded having a grandad just like him.

The Census lady called back the following Friday.

'I can't tell you how many people make mistakes on these forms, but this is perfect,' she said.

The relief was massive. So was the thought that in one hundred years someone might wonder about William Dearborne and his grandson Martin, but it would take some detective to figure it out.

I had to go back to my mother's house one last time. I found a key for the back door, so I patched up the kitchen window a bit and locked up. Then I caught the bus back to Ballincollig. It was a Monday morning so I hoped my stepfather would be out. He was at home, in stained pyjamas, watching TV, when I arrived. 'What you doing here, you little pup?' he said. I said nothing, just went upstairs and searched in Mam's room until I found my birth certificate and everything else I thought I'd need. 'You can fuck right off,' was all he said as I was leaving.

On the day I turned eighteen, I woke up early to get to the dole office and be first in line. It was pelting rain outside, but I didn't care. All I wanted was to fill out the forms and get myself sorted. I was a man now and a small bit of rain wouldn't hurt me.

Back at Liberty Terrace, I checked the street until the coast was clear, then I snuck round the back of Number 10 as usual and used the key to open the kitchen door. I made myself a cheese and onion sandwich and a cup of tea and got stuck into another detective book. I was just at a good bit where the private eye was getting off with a woman he called a dame when I heard the front door opening. Next thing, an old white-haired fella was standing in the kitchen staring at me.

'Who the fuck are you?' he said.

When I stood up, I knocked over the cup of tea. I would have run out the back door only I was too scared to move.

It was William Dearborne and he had his fists up, ready to punch me.

'I thought you were dead,' I said.

'Christ almighty, who told you I was dead?' He looked fierce tough for an old fella.

'Sorry,' I said. 'I heard a man in Liberty Terrace conked out from a stroke and I thought it was you.'

He lowered his fists and stared hard at me.

'I was sleeping rough, so I figured there was an empty house... I only needed a place til I could get the dole.'

'You little bollocks,' he said. 'Sit down there. I'm going to call the Guards.'

But he stood there, looking at me, instead of picking up the old-fashioned phone right there on the kitchen table. Then he said, 'What age are you anyway?'

'Eighteen,' I said. 'Today's my birthday.'

'Well, birthday boy, you've made a right mess of my house.'

I looked around and saw that he was right. My mother would have killed me if she'd seen the state of the place. She was always on at me about tidying up after myself. I'd patched up the broken window with a bit of plywood but it looked like what it was, a total bodge job. There were dirty plates in the sink, a greasy frying pan on the hob, bottles, cans, crusts and crumbs on the kitchen counter. On the table, congealed microwave containers, a carton of milk, the remains of the Tesco's Finest Lasagne I'd had for breakfast.

'Well,' he said. 'You're not leaving until you've cleared up after you.'

He still had a fierce look on his face, but it seemed like he wasn't going to call the cops. So I did exactly what I was told. I gathered all the rubbish and put it in the bin. Then he made me get a cloth and wipe down all the surfaces. He ordered me to get the vacuum cleaner from under the stairs (I never knew there was one) and made me hoover all the downstairs, then all the upstairs and then I had to wash the kitchen floor. He made me put the towels in the washing machine and he'd have had made me wash the bedlinen as well, he said, but it was obvious I'd slept on the couch. He asked me all sorts of questions in between barking out orders, and I told him whatever he wanted to know. By the time I was finished I was knackered but at least Mr. Dearborne wasn't as furious as he'd been in the beginning. He was cranky all right, but he wasn't a bastard.

'Right,' he said then. 'I could murder some fish and chips. You, go off to Jackie Lennox's and get two fish suppers with mushy peas. And some drink from the Offie across the road.' He hesitated. 'A big bottle of 7-Up maybe.'

He handed me €30 and told me to get my ass back pronto before the chips got cold. I ran most of the way there and raced back even faster, the warm bundle of food in one hand, a bottle of 7-Up in a plastic bag in the other.

When I got back, I pressed the front doorbell once, like a normal person, and he came out and raised his eyebrows before he let me back in.

We sat at the kitchen table while he took out plates and knives and forks, ketchup, salt and vinegar. He put the food on the plates and poured 7-Up into two glasses. He told me to eat my supper while it was hot, like Mam used to do.

'You must have run fast,' he said.

'I did, Mr. Dearborne. Thanks for the food.'

'It's a good chipper,' he said.

It was. The fish in batter was melt in the mouth, the chips were proper chips and the mushy peas were just the job.

'I phoned Bernice Callinan,' said Mr. Dearborne, in between bites. 'She told me Albert Clarke from Number 1 is in a coma. Locked-in-Syndrome, is what they call it. He might as well be dead, apparently.'

He forked another chip, dipped it into the pool of ketchup on his plate and shoved it in his mouth.

I stopped eating. I wasn't sure what to say. I'd picked the wrong house. Maybe my stepfather had a point. Only a complete thick could make such a balls of it.

Mr. Dearborne swallowed another mouthful of food and reached for his glass.

'There was something rotten about Albert,' he said. 'I didn't like him. But even so, it's a terrible thing.' Then he smiled at me. 'At least I'm still alive and kicking.'

It was then and only then it dawned on me that he was exactly the same William Dearborne as the one that I had in my head all along.

'Sorry for giving you a fright,' I said. 'I never meant to.'

'Apology accepted.' He lifted his glass and looked me straight in the eye. 'Cheers,' he said.

I raised my glass as he bumped his gently against mine.

'I'll pay for the broken window. Honestly. And the stuff I used.'

He took another slug of 7-Up and put his glass down. He turned his head to glance around the kitchen. It looked better now than when I broke in, apart from the busted window.

'And how will you do that?'

'Begging,' I said. My stepfather always asked trick questions, but I figured Mr. Dearborne wasn't like him and I'd be as well off to tell the truth.

He frowned.

'Only until I get my dole. She said it would take maybe two weeks.'

He forked a bit of fish and dipped it in the tartare sauce, but he didn't eat it. He just stared at it a while. The silence kind of got to me, so I tried to think of something to say. I remembered that he used to have a dog.

'Do you like dogs, Mr. Dearborne?' I asked by way of conversation.

'Yes, I do. I loved my dog.' He put his fork down and looked as if he was thinking about Rusty.

'I guessed you had one, because of the collar and lead out in the hall. We had a dog once too. I was only small then, but I was mad about him.'

He stretched his legs out under the table and sat back in his chair.

'I should have got another dog after Rusty,' he said. 'But I couldn't bear to. I was afraid I'd get too fond of the next dog and then he'd die and then I'd be alone again, and I'd feel even worse.'

He sighed then and looked across the table at me for what seemed like a long time. Then he spoke.

'Would you like to stay here until you get sorted?' He looked down again at his plate of food and waited.

The kitchen was warm, and my belly was full, and I had nowhere else to go. But still, I could hardly believe my luck.

'Could I really?' I said.

'Sure, it'll tide you over anyway.' He looked up at me again, then picked up his glass of 7-Up, looked at it and put it down again.

'Thanks a million, Mr. Dearborne.' I said, and I meant it.

'Call me William,' he said. 'One thing though. You can't go out begging while you're here.'

I thought about that for a minute. 'I could do some jobs around the place for you, earn my keep, like. Go to the shops and do the hoovering.'

'It's a deal,' he said.

'If you got a dog, I could walk the dog for you.'

'I suppose you could,' said William.

THE CALLINANS WENT TO PARIS

Bernice stood in her mother's bedroom, holding a large bottle of body lotion aloft in her right hand. Her mother, Mrs. Vivienne Callinan, sat on the bed, both arms folded and her general demeanour that of a sulky teenager caught smoking. She was wearing her best coat and a matching scarf. A carry-on suitcase sat next to Mrs. Callinan, its contents spilling out onto the duvet.

'I told you already, you can only bring liquids of 100 ml or less,' Bernice said.

'Sure, they'll never notice, if I wrap it up in my dressing gown.' Mrs. Callinan, arms still folded, shrugged her shoulders and looked up at Bernice.

'They would.' Bernice placed the bottle of body lotion firmly on her mother's dressing table. 'Look, we can buy you some in the Duty Free,' she said, turning her attention back to the suitcase. 'Or when we get there.'

'I've paid for our flights, haven't I? I should be able to take what I want,' Mrs. Callinan said, fingering her scarf.

'It's to prevent terrorists from blowing up the plane.' Bernice opened her mouth to say something else but thought better of it. Instead, she rolled up a jumper and placed it carefully back in the case.

Downstairs, the front doorbell rang.

'Oh God, that must be the taxi,' said Bernice. She raced out of the bedroom and shouted down the stairs.

'Colin, will you answer the door? If it's the taxi, tell him to wait a few minutes.'

Colin was Bernice's only sibling. The only job she'd asked of him was to keep an eye out for the taxi.

She returned to her mother's bedroom and began to hurriedly repack the bag. This was the third time she had had to edit her mother's luggage. The first was two weeks ago when her mother had shown her a large suitcase filled with enough items to see her through an Arctic voyage. The second was last week when Bernice supplied her with a smart carry-on case. The third was today, shortly before they were due to leave for the airport. They were only going to Paris for the weekend.

'I think it's a disgrace.' Mrs. Callinan sat, unmoving.

The doorbell rang again.

'Why doesn't he answer the bloody door?' said Bernice. 'I specifically asked him.'

'Ah, he'll get there in a minute,' her mother said.

'Right,' said Bernice. She placed her mother's fluffy dressing-gown on top of everything else, pushed down the lid and forced the zipper closed. As she shoved a plastic bag of travel-sized toiletries into her mother's handbag, the doorbell rang again three times, urgently.

'I'll come back in a minute and carry down your case,' Bernice said, over her shoulder, to her mother, before running down the stairs.

Bernice almost tripped over her own small, slightly battered Samsonite in her rush to open the front door. A tired-looking woman stood on the doorstep. She wore a yellow fluorescent jacket over a black raincoat. A heavy-looking black bag hung over her shoulder and she held a bulky notepad on a clipboard.

'Hello,' she said. 'Sorry to bother you. I'm calling about the Census.'

Bernice looked past her to check the taxi's whereabouts.

The woman held up the badge that hung from a lanyard round her neck. 'I just need to give you a form and ask you a few questions.'

Bernice turned back to peer at the ID. It looked official, though the photo could have been of any middle-aged female.

'Honestly, I don't have time for this.' Bernice looked pointedly at the watch on her wrist, a big old Timex that had belonged to her late father.

'No problem,' the woman said. 'This is Number 5, Liberty Terrace, isn't it?'

'Yes,' said Bernice.

'Great. I'll just give you the form, so. How many people live here?'

'My mother and my brother,' Bernice said. 'I'm only staying here temporarily. I'm hoping to be out of here before Census Day.' Before I go out of my mind, she added, but only to herself.

The Census lady wrote something hurriedly on her clipboard.

'Look,' said Bernice. 'We're just about to leave for the airport.'

'Right, sorry, well, here's the form you'll need to fill out.'

Bernice accepted the form and plonked it on the hall table inside the door, just as a taxi glided to a halt on the street outside the house.

Mrs. Callinan slowly descended the stairs, calling out, 'I'm nearly ready now. Who's this?'

Bernice waved at the taxi driver and gave him a thumb's up, before turning back to her mother who was standing in the hall. 'It's about the Census. Would you ever find Colin, tell him the taxi's here?'

'I will, as soon as I find the case for my glasses.' Mrs. Callinan ambled off into the sitting room.

'Would you mind giving me a contact number?' the Census lady asked.

'Oh for God's sake,' Bernice muttered. She recited her mobile number to the Census lady, who scribbled it on her pad and headed off down the path.

'We'll be out in two minutes,' Bernice told the taxi driver, before running inside to search for her brother.

Colin was sitting in the back garden, leisurely smoking a cigarette.

'The taxi's waiting,' she said.

'All right, all right. I'll be there in a minute. Is Ma ready?'

'Yes,' said Bernice. She had found her mother's glasses case on the kitchen counter.

'I'll just finish my fag and I'll be in.'

'Right. Remember to lock the back door before we leave.'

Once Colin and her mother and the luggage were all safely installed in the taxi, Bernice had second thoughts. 'Wait a second,' she said and ran inside again to double-check. Just as well she did. The back door had not been locked. Back in the taxi, she bit her lip and decided to say nothing.

On the plane, Bernice studied the laminated card of instructions on what to do in the event of a crash landing.

Then she watched the flight attendant's limp rendition of what to do in an emergency, how to inflate the yellow lifejacket, where the attached whistle was located, how to pull down the oxygen tube. Nothing remotely dangerous had ever happened to Bernice. Nothing momentous ever happened to her, she thought. Even her marriage had been mundane, and its decline had been a slow, inexorable process, flattening her bit by bit, like pastry under a rolling pin, as she tried to ignore how thin she was being stretched.

Now, as she looked out through the tiny window at nothing but clouds, Bernice knew she should never have agreed to the trip. But at the time, surrounded by the ruins of her marriage, she'd been caught off-guard.

'Just you and me, dear. I never get to go anywhere. I'll pay,' Mrs. Callinan had said, munificently. At least it would be a weekend away from Colin, Bernice had thought. A week later, her mother had said, quite casually, that she was bringing Colin too. He needs a break, the poor divil, she had said.

Colin lost his most recent job two years ago. 'Due to the recession,' his mother said, but Bernice felt sure that Colin's errant moods, his unreliability and his drinking had more than likely put him top of the list for redundancy and that the directors of the insurance company had been glad of the excuse to let him go. Not to mention the cocaine. Six months later their father died and Colin moved back home, ostensibly to care for the newly widowed Mrs. Callinan. All the neighbours and all Mrs. Callinan's friends — everyone, it seemed — thought this was quite heroic. Bernice did not.

Mrs. Callinan, sitting next to her, had fallen asleep soon after the plane took off, as if determined to ignore her current whereabouts, and was making small snoring sounds, while Colin, in the aisle seat, flicked through the in-flight magazine, resolutely giving the impression that he was travelling alone.

The security at Charles De Gaulle Airport seemed to be on red alert. A group of CRS police in dark blue uniforms paced through the terminal, their black rifles dangling like extra limbs, their gilets helpfully branded with the word 'Police' on the back. Two other police officers followed in different uniforms. A third was tugged along by an Alsatian straining on its leash.

'Sniffer dog,' said Colin. 'Lucky I don't have any drugs on me.'

'So many Gardaí,' Mrs. Callinan said, peering anxiously around her as they waited in line to go through customs. 'Bernice, I feel as weak as water all of a sudden. Would you be able to manage my suitcase as well as your own?'

'You do look a bit pale,' said Bernice. She slung her handbag round her neck and dragged her mother's suitcase as well as her own, leading Mrs. Callinan and Colin all the way through customs and crowded corridors until they finally exited the terminal and found a taxi rank.

Afterwards, at the hotel, Bernice found out why her mother had become unsettled. Mrs. Callinan had managed to slip the 500 ml bottle of her favourite body lotion into her suitcase after all. It was tucked into one of her slippers.

That evening, the Callinans went out to dinner. The restaurant — on rue du Faubourg Montmartre — was already busy, despite the early hour. The perfectly-preserved interior resembled a 1920's dining hall, with tall mirrored walls, glass globe light fittings and brass coat-racks suspended above the wooden tables. The tables themselves were covered in red gingham, with white paper tablecloths on top.

The bustling waiters wore black waistcoats and white aprons. They dashed around writing customers' orders in blue pen on the white paper tablecloths and rushed back and forth with glasses, bottles, cutlery and plates of food.

Bernice sat at the short end of the table on a bentwood chair. From there she could see the front entrance, where a group of American tourists waited with their tour guide, to be seated. It was early for dinner by French standards, only 6.30 p.m., and she wasn't very hungry, but she knew that her mother was keeping Irish time.

Colin sat at the opposite end of the table to Bernice and stared past her head at the ornate bar at the back of the room. Earlier, after they had booked into the hotel, he'd disappeared, leaving Bernice to settle their mother in the room and stay with her while she had her nap. He had turned up in time to go for dinner, but he seemed unusually quiet. Bernice hoped he hadn't managed to buy some weed and that he was simply tired.

Mrs. Callinan was ensconced on the leather-covered banquette seat with her back to the wall, so that she could survey her surroundings.

'What are you going to order?' Mrs. Callinan asked. She held her menu at arm's length in front of her and peered at it with some difficulty, even though a pair of glasses hung from her neck on a chain.

'I don't know,' said Bernice. Paris had been a place she had been happy in, once, long ago. She had spent one daring year here as an au pair—and might have stayed if a failed affair with an Algerian barman had not flattened her. Instead, she returned home, heart-scalded, to a secure and more appropriate job in the County Hall. Soon afterwards, she met her husband and felt grateful to be wanted. Before she married him and regretted it. Before the ostensibly civil divorce proceedings and the sale of their house.

She had been scrupulously fair as regards the financial issues — in fact she'd overdone it, so desperate was she to put an end to the thing. Although she'd provided the deposit, she'd insisted the (too small) profit from the sale should be divided right down the middle. Anything to avoid conflict, to get it over and done with. The small apartment she was buying would be a new, clean start. It was unfortunate that the sale had had to complete before her purchase could. A month's delay or more. The cheapest option, at the time, was to move into her mother's house temporarily. Too late (again) she realised what a terrible mistake she'd made. She'd forgotten what living with her mother was like, and now, without her father's tempering presence Mrs. Callinan was even worse — and as for Bernice's brother... Oh brother. My useless brother. Honestly, sometimes she felt like murdering the pair of them.

'Well, let's ask for a bottle of the house white anyway,' suggested Mrs. Callinan. 'And maybe some water?'

'Good idea, Mother.' Bernice looked up at the waiter. 'Ah, Monsieur, une bouteille de vin blanc, s'il vous plait, le vin maison, je pense, et...' She looked quickly at her mother and at Colin, who was frowning at the tablecloth. 'Will we get sparkling water?' Her mother nodded. 'Et de l'eau gazeuse aussi. Merci bien.'

The waiter took a pen from behind his ear and wrote two numbers on the paper tablecloth before departing.

'Actually,' Colin looked up from the table and stared at Bernice. 'You could have waited a second there before you started showing off your French. I mean, I might have had something to say, if only you'd let me get a word in edgeways.'

'Oh, sorry about that. Do you want a coke or something?

I'll order it as soon as he comes back.'

'Whatever,' Colin grunted as he rose from his seat. 'I need a slash.'

He walked off in the direction of an illuminated red and white sign across the room that read 'Toilettes'. A staircase led down to toilets in the basement, Bernice realised, as Colin seemed to disappear downwards bit by bit until only the back of his head could be seen, and then nothing.

Mrs. Callinan frowned at the cutlery in front of her on the table and began to straighten it. The herd of American tourists were ushered in by a waiter, who settled them at the long table next to theirs.

'Well, this is a very nice restaurant,' Mrs. Callinan said. 'It's exactly how I imagined it would be.'

'I thought Colin would like it here, seeing as he's so into Proust and all that.' Bernice put her hand to her mouth and concentrated on biting the skin of her index finger.

'I know he can be difficult,' admitted Mrs. Callinan. 'But sometimes I feel you provoke him on purpose.'

'If he acted like a normal human being, we wouldn't have to walk on egg shells around him all the time,' Bernice said loudly, so that she could be heard above the loud babble of the Americans.

'Now, for my sake, darling, won't you make an effort with your brother when he comes back?'

'Oh brother,' said Bernice. You ain't heavy, you're just my unbelievably unbearable, dysfunctional big brother.

Mrs. Callinan opened her mouth again but said nothing because the elderly waiter had appeared alongside their table, an ice bucket in his hand, the ice clinking against a bottle of wine. Bernice watched him as he placed it on the table and uncorked the bottle, before pouring a little into her mother's glass. 'He expects you to taste it to see if it's okay,' she told her mother. Mrs. Callinan tasted it, nodded and smiled. The waiter refilled her glass and poured wine into Bernice's glass. She covered the third glass with her hand and the waiter hesitated, before replacing the bottle in the ice bucket and moving away.

Bernice tasted the wine as she studied the menu. Behind her, she heard one of the American ladies ask how safe it was to walk around at night. The tour guide's voice could be heard, his English tinted with his native French. 'Much safer now, since last year... there are security cameras all around the city now, like in London.' Then she could hear no more above a rush of chatter from an English family of four who were settling at another table nearby. She was beginning to wonder if it was a deliberate move on the waiting staff's part to lumber all the annoying foreigners together in this section and occupy the other side of the room with sleeker, more sophisticated Parisians.

Mrs. Callinan held the bottle up and studied the label. 'Lovely bottle,' she said.

Bernice looked up. 'Yeah,' she said. 'Nice.'

'What do you think of the wine?' asked her mother.

'Delicious,' said Bernice. 'I'm feeling better already.'

'Sláinte,' said her mother, as she touched Bernice's glass with her own.

Colin weaved his way back across the room and flopped into his chair, without looking at Bernice or his mother.

'Do you want a coke or something?' Bernice asked, in a level tone.

'No.' Carefully, he poured wine into the third wine glass right up to the rim. He swigged it back and when he replaced his glass on the table it was almost empty.

'It's corked,' he said.

Bernice looked at him despairingly. 'I was hoping you

wouldn't start.'

'Don't you think it's corked?' he asked.

'Do you think it's corked, Mother?' asked Bernice.

'It seems fine to me,' said Mrs. Callinan.

'Anyway, who cares?' asked Colin, looking directly at Bernice. 'It's alcohol.' He took the bottle and refilled his glass, then leaned over to top all three glasses up.

'Well, this is nice, isn't it?' Mrs. Callinan said.

'Glad you approve,' Bernice replied, in a very calm voice. She tried to keep the expression on her face blank.

'It tastes like a pretty decent white to me,' said Mrs. Callinan. She reached for the bottle again and sniffed the open top, before examining the label as if she might find some kind of clue. The wine was almost gone.

'The house white in French restaurants is usually pretty good,' said Bernice.

'Yes, that's what I've always heard,' said Mrs. Callinan, looking vaguely around the room.

'So, since you and I have no problem, Mother, and we all know Colin isn't supposed to drink, why are we wasting time when we could be ordering some food?' said Bernice. 'And why don't you stop looking at me like that, Colin?'

'You started it. I saw the way you looked at him just now,' said Mrs. Callinan.

'Oh God, not this again,' said Bernice. 'Look, let's just check out the menu and decide what to order.' She scanned the menu hurriedly, trying to figure out the easiest route towards getting her mother to make up her mind.

'Yes, let's do that,' said Mrs. Callinan, but instead of reading her menu she looked around again at her surroundings. 'It's so lovely and French here, isn't it?' she observed. 'All the lovely lights and mirrors and everything. Has it always been like this?'

'Well, it's been a restaurant for over a hundred years I

think,' said Bernice. 'But it's been French for — oh — centuries, I'd say.'

'I always longed to travel the world,' Mrs. Callinan sighed. 'Of course, I never had the advantages in life you had.' She looked at Bernice when she said this. 'I met your father and we married far too young. And then you came along, Colin, and you cried all day and all night for two years — and just when Colin finally decided to sleep for more than two hours at a stretch, you arrived, Bernice. There are whole years of my life I can't remember now — I was so exhausted from the pair of you. And travel, well, that was out of the question. We didn't have the money at first and then, when we did, your father would never go anywhere anyway. God rest his soul.'

Poor Dad, thought Bernice. Such a quiet man. Perhaps because he couldn't get a word in edgeways. He'd died of cancer, a rotten cancer, and all she had left of him was the Timex watch on her wrist. He'd been the constant taxi driver for the family, since Mrs. Callinan had never learnt to drive. She could recall his profile now, as he sat patiently in the driver's seat, reading one of his books. He had spent so much time waiting in his Ford Sierra. A long time waiting for Mrs. Callinan to emerge from the shops, from the hair salon, from the beautician. Waiting for Colin after GAA matches. Waiting for both of them to finish music lessons, swimming lessons, exams. Waiting for Bernice at the airport when she came home. Waiting for Mrs. Callinan to return from her pilgrimages to Lourdes, Fatima and Rome. He hadn't travelled far himself, but perhaps he'd travelled in his head.

Mrs. Callinan held her menu out at arm's length once more. She felt for her glasses which still dangled at her bosom. She put them on, then held the menu at a normal distance. She began to move her lips as she read.

'It's all very French, isn't it?' she said. 'I don't see anything on this menu I'd like to eat.'

'I'm having salade verte — that's basically lettuce salad — and then chicken and chips,' Bernice said, putting her menu down. 'There's French Onion soup too, Mam. You like soup, don't you?'

'So, let's get on with it,' said Colin. He shut his menu, slapped it down on the table and waved at the elderly waiter, who came over and looked at him questioningly.

'Another one, please,' said Colin, holding up the bottle of wine towards the waiter. His face already glowed with false contentment.

'Sure, you only live once,' her mother said, with a warning look at Bernice.

Bernice knew that Colin had out-manouevred her. It was weird to get a sense of dèjâ vu in France — or perhaps this was the perfect place to experience it. The errant behaviour was only just beginning. She'd bite her tongue this one last time, but she'd avoid getting into these situations altogether from now on. Better late than never, her therapist had said.

'You're right,' she said. 'Let's push the boat out.'

Colin looked at her quizzically, as if regretting the lost opportunity for strife. Bernice was reminded of her ex-husband. Perhaps, as her therapist had suggested, she had married her husband only because his behaviour had seemed so familiar; that he was part of a pattern she needed to avoid — a tendency to accept bad behaviour for the sake of peace.

The waiter still stood before them, so Bernice ordered her starter and main course.

'Tell him I'll have the soup and the chicken,' said Mrs. Callinan.

Bernice did.

'Agneau is lamb, isn't it?' Colin asked.

'You're right,' she said, relieved that she didn't have to

contradict him.

'I'll have the paté foie gras and the lamb,' Colin refilled his glass with wine and slugged it back.

By the time the main courses arrived, Colin had drunk most of the second bottle of wine and ordered another one.

'I mean, they were a complete bunch of tossers,' he said of his former employers. 'It's a wonder they haven't shut up shop altogether.'

'I don't think I can manage a dessert,' said Bernice.

'Me neither,' he said affably. 'I'll have a brandy.'

'Do you really...' Bernice hesitated.

Colin's eyes glittered as he stared at her, and for a moment she felt scared. Why did he hate her so much? What had become of him? Once she had admired him; loved him, even.

'I might have apple tart if they have it,' said Mrs. Callinan. 'Bernice, see if they have apple tart.'

Colin filled his glass and drank again.

After some consultation, Bernice ordered tea for her mother and a peach melba since there was no apple tart. She ordered coffee for herself and a double brandy for her brother. Colin nodded almost benignly. 'Right, I'll be back in a minute,' he said, and he wended his way unsteadily towards the toilets, barely managing to avoid collisions.

'I can't believe this,' said Bernice. 'You let him get away with everything. You always have.'

'Ah Bernice, don't make a fuss. He needs to let his hair down a bit.'

'Does he?'

'Ah Bernice, you have to make allowances.' She blinked and looked down at her plate. 'He was so bright as a young lad. Your father was so proud of him. It's not his fault he has a nervous disposition.'

Nervous disposition, my foot, thought Bernice. When Colin was in the drying-out clinic, Mrs. Callinan told everyone he was in hospital with diptheria.

'I mean you were a good girl, Bernice. You always worked so hard,' Mrs. Callinan continued. 'There you were studying all hours, and you made such an effort, always, in fairness, but Colin, he was so smart he hardly had to work at all in school.'

That was part of the trouble, Bernice realised. He'd been so good at everything — almost too good — until she came along and turned out to be, occasionally, better. She remembered the swimming lessons, when she was seven and Colin was ten. Mrs. Doherty, the teacher, had been fat and a bit cross; Colin joked to Bernice that Mrs. Doherty's blubber alone would keep her afloat, and that made Bernice giggle and feel less afraid of her. She and Colin had been friends then. She had looked up to her big brother. A wave of pure sadness assailed her. Colin could swim the length of the pool while Bernice was still holding desperately onto a blue kickboard, propelling herself anxiously along the pool wall, holding her head out of the water. By the time she'd managed a clumsy breaststroke, he was already learning to dive. She'd never be as good as him at swimming, she knew, but how proud she'd felt, all the same, when he flew off the diving board and how relieved she was to see him emerge in triumph from the depths, shaking water off his hair like a dog. He'd been fearless, her valiant big brother.

Now she could see Colin's head gradually appear, as he came up the stairs from the toilets — and she watched, alarmed, as he stumbled on the top step and only narrowly recovered his balance. Oh God, he's totally pissed, she thought and hoped they would get him back to the hotel without too much aggravation.

It was then that Bernice heard a panicked voice saying something in French — some pleading, begging words — and suddenly the whoosh of chatter crested into quiet. She turned her head back towards the restaurant's entrance where a waiter, still as a statue, held his hands up in surrender. A man dressed in black stood next to him, a gun in his hand, a black mask covering most of his face, except for his eyes. Though later Bernice wondered if she'd imagined it, in her memory the gunman's eyes stared straight into hers with a look of pure hatred and for a moment they were her brother's eyes, as they had stared at her earlier in the evening, and she remembered the gunman saying something that she did not understand and she wanted to scream as Colin stood stock-still in the middle of the room while everyone else in the restaurant was dropping to the ground and that he stared straight at the gunman and said, 'Who the fuck do you think you are? What's going on here?'

But while the gunman aimed straight at Colin, Bernice didn't scream, only whisper 'Get down Mam, get down' while Mrs. Callinan fumbled with the glasses round her neck and sat there, staring at her son. All Bernice remembered, afterwards, was falling on the floor and bursts of gunfire and something heavy falling on her and shrieks and more gunshots and then a pause and then another round of fire and it seemed a long, long time before the shooting stopped, and all around her was the sound of panicked voices, sobbing, muttered prayers, then louder and louder wailing as the sirens blared.

Some weeks later, back in Ireland, Bernice was in her mother's house when the doorbell rang. It was lunchtime but Bernice was still in her pyjamas and dressing gown. The Census lady stood on the doorstep, damp in yellow jacket, black bag slung over her shoulder, clipboard and pen in hand, hair drizzled damp from a recent shower of rain.

'Sorry to bother you,' she said. 'I'm here to collect your form.'

Bernice took the neatly filled-out form from the hall table.

'I need to quickly check,' the Census lady said. 'Sorry about this but you wouldn't believe... you see, any errors and I'll only have to come back again.' She looked at the form and then at the notepad on her clipboard. She hesitated and then spoke again. 'I made a note when I called the first time that three people lived here, so I have to ask...'

'Only one now. My mother and my brother were killed in Paris a few weeks ago. The night of the terrorist attacks.'

The Census woman's face flushed. She looked as if she was about to cry. 'I'm so, so sorry. What a terrible tragedy. I saw it on the news. You must be in bits.' She hesitated. 'He was a hero, though. That must give you some comfort.'

Colin's photo had been plastered all over the media, both in Ireland and abroad. He had been valiant, fearless, the journalists said. One headline read:

Heroic Irishman tried to reason with lone gunman.

Mrs. Callinan would have been proud as punch, had she been alive, herself, to read the headlines.

'Yes,' said Bernice to the Census lady. 'A hero. So they tell me.' She closed the door firmly and stomped upstairs. She was fed up of feeling angry, feeling guilty, and sometimes feeling nothing but a terrible heaviness in her bones. Even at the funerals she had felt like a bit-part player in a dreadful disaster movie, longing but unable to change her scripted lines. At least the house was hers now, or would be, as soon as the solicitor completed the probate. She could sell it, go and live in her brand-new apartment. Or she could sell the apartment and stay here, in Liberty Terrace. She could take time off work or even change career. She could do whatever she wanted, if only she knew what that was. She showered and dressed in an old pair of jeans and a sweater. She strapped her father's watch on her wrist, and saw it was already two o'clock.

The small suitcase Bernice had bought for her mother still lay, unpacked, on the upstairs landing. Bernice took a deep breath and grabbed it. In Mrs. Callinan's bedroom she unzipped the case and held it open over Mrs. Callinan's bed. The contents fell haphazardly on top of the duvet and her mother's body lotion rolled out and onto the carpet.

Bernice picked up the bottle and twisted open the top. She squeezed some of the lotion out, rubbed it on her wrist and sniffed at it a couple of times. Then she took the bottle into the bathroom and squeezed the contents viciously into the toilet bowl. She flushed the toilet and creamy blobs of congealed lotion swirled round and round in the bowl until they were finally sluiced away. Then she threw the almost empty bottle of lotion in the bin.

QUALITY TIME

If only one of those idiot nurses would turn his television on. All he had to contemplate was the ceiling above him. That dreadful ceiling, with its banal magnolia paint. Supreme blandness, but for a daub in a slightly darker shade right above his bed. An oddly-shaped imperfection — the result, he was convinced, of something more sinister — blood from an exploding vein, a leaping spurt of pus, an ejaculation? The reason for the overlay of paint obsessed him daily since he'd found himself stretched out on this hospital bed, helpless and utterly immobile.

The multiple ignominies of the past week made him seethe with impotent fury but at least the lackeys had not overlooked his Laya GoldPlus health insurance, so he had a private room. His field of vision was limited to the upper part of the door on his left and of the window on the right, that dratted ceiling, the helpless emergency cord dangling like a neglected toy barely visible in the corner of his eye, and — thankfully — the television hanging on its metal limb high up on the far wall.

On duty today was the one he called Nurse Wretched. He could hear her now, outside the half-open door, talking primly to some bint about filling out a form. 'Yes, indeed, Albert Clarke, Number 1 Liberty Terrace,' he heard her say, all prissy-like. 'Lived alone, his neighbour said. He can't speak — or sign the form, obviously.'

If only he could speak, he'd have a thing or two to say to Nurse Wretched, the silly bitch. He detested all the nurses, in fact, except for little Nursie Tinybones with her soft plump hands and incongruous scent of bubblegum and flowers. And Patchett, the physio, was not a bad sort — at least she provided the only smidgeon of bodily ease he'd experienced since that blasted stroke.

If only bloody Nurse Wretched would switch the dratted TV on. The careless cow had also left his door ajar. He could hear the enervating clatter of the underlings outside and smell some disastrous boiled vegetable-ness floating in the disinfectant air. Even more excruciating was Wretched's fake-sincere chatter with some female in the corridor outside.

'So here he is and won't he be delighted to see you, the poor poppet!' Nurse Wretched squealed as she swung round the door and into the room, hovering over him, showing him off as if he were Exhibit A.

'Now look who's come all the way from London to see her dear old Dad!' she cooed.

If only Wretched would drop dead.

'Thank you, Nurse.' The other woman's voice seemed unaccountably familiar, despite the slight English accent.

'He can't turn his head, dear. You'll have to get in close so he'll see you.'

A middle-aged woman leaned over him. There was something distinctly recognisable about her.

'So... this is a Diving Bell and Butterfly scenario, is it?' asked the woman in her Englishy accent.

'What?'

'Am I correct to assume that he knows what's going on even though he can't move or speak or... well, do anything?'

'He can move his eyes, dear, but that's all. That's how we know he likes to watch the telly.'

The English woman looked at him and he rolled both his eyes at her.

There. See what you make of that, girlie. See what you make of that.

'And all these tubes?'

'Well, pet, he can't breathe properly without them. We have to feed him intravenously as well.' Nurse Wretched lowers her voice. 'He has to wear an incontinence pad down below, of course.'

'And you don't know how long this condition will last?'

'No, dear... well I'm not allowed to say. You'll have to talk to the Consultant.'

'I understand. Thank you.'

'Right then. I'll leave you to it.'

Exit Nurse Wretched. The door clunked shut behind her.

The English woman leaned over, so that he could see her face again.

'Well, well, Dad,' she said. 'Long time no see. It's me, Trisha.'

Yes, it was his daughter, Trisha. He recognised those bitter little eyes, the bone structure of her face, the still-beautiful hair. She must be almost forty now, he supposed. Well-preserved, all the same. The lovely smooth blonde hair— a shame she wore it shorter now—what was the name of that style? A bob? The outfit was pitiful; somewhat like the clothes that Wifey used to wear. A blue denim jacket over a white blouse. Did they still call them blouses? Cheap dangly earrings. No class. How could she? Wifey had no class either. In the end, he had despised Wifey. Though not as much as she despised him, he supposed. He blinked. *I'm still here girlie. See what you make of that.*

Trisha looked almost afraid, but she recovered within moments. 'You're in there all right, aren't you? You're still there, Dad. Not that you deserve to be.'

The colour of his daughter's hair was darker than he recalled. Ash blond, was it? In his memory, she was a fairytale child with long golden tresses. From this rancid bedtrap he could still imagine — almost feel — the smooth ripeness of her hair.

'Trust you to have great health insurance. Just as well, I suppose. You're going to be here for a long time.' She walked around the bed and from the other side she leaned over again to peer into his face.

'Can you hear me?' she asked, loudly. She looked into his eyes. 'You're in there all right, you bastard. Yes, it's me, your daughter. Let's spend some quality time together, shall we?' She straightened up and walked back around the bed. She sat down in the chair. He could barely see her now, but he could smell a faint lemony perfume.

'Hilarious that you can't talk,' she said, in a hard voice. 'You used to have plenty to say, didn't you? Hardly ever stopped ranting at Mum and upsetting her. When you were in the house, the only time we had peace was when you read to me. But the books you chose — I couldn't understand half of them. Remember Don Quixote? Tilting at windmills. I had no idea what it was all about. I was probably only four then. I just listened. I'd do anything to keep you in a good mood.'

He remembered, quite suddenly and clearly, the cover of that book: a daft old man on a horse, wearing yellow armour;

and little Sancho Panza, his underling, bound to obey a lunatic who was out of control. The tale had amused him once.

'I remember the way you brushed my hair and counted. Forty slow brushstrokes on each section and then you'd... Oh God...' She put her head in her hands.

He thought she might be crying. What the heck was she fussing about?

'I wish Mum could see you now — the state of you — but she can't. She's dead. She died last year. Did you know that? I didn't bother letting you know. It should have been you who died.' She wiped her eyes.

He heard the door open. Nurse Minny Mouse squeaked in, all pert and businessy as usual.

'Just got to do his bloods,' she chirped.

How he hated them all.

At his side he felt, rather than saw, Trisha rising from the chair.

'No need to move,' Nurse Minny Mouse said. 'You can stay if you like. So long as you're not squeamish.'

'No, I'm not a bit squeamish. Thank you, Nurse.'

He felt her sit down again, a small flow of air and that lemon fragrance, with a hint of flowers, perhaps lilies.

'You're the daughter, aren't you? Call me Barbara,' Mousey said cheerfully, as she jabbed a needle most painfully into the flesh of his upper arm. How he longed to roar at that despicable woman. All her pernickety tidiness and yet she was clueless about the most basic of tasks. That small rodent face of hers was asking to be hit.

'I hear you only just arrived from London,' said Mousey to his daughter. 'You must be exhausted. I could bring you a cup of tea, if you like?'

'That's very kind of you, but I'm fine, thanks.'

'So whereabouts in London do you live?'

He wished Mousey would quit sticking her nosy little nose in. He hated her even more than Nurse Wretched now.

'Muswell Hill.'

'That's North London, isn't it? I used to live in Clapham once upon a time.'

'I lived there too, for a while, when I was ten. Then my mother met my stepfather, so we moved to North London when I was twelve.'

From his stodgy static bed he felt intensely vexed. So Wifey had met someone else, the bitch? Surely it couldn't have lasted.

'And do you come back to Ireland very often?'

'Not really,' said Trisha.

'Well, at least you're here now, that's the main thing, isn't it?' Nurse Minnie Mouse squeaked.

He could not see what the nurse was doing but he could hear her fannying about beside him, probably fixing adhesive labels on the vials of his still-warm blood.

'Yes,' said his daughter, absently.

The nurse fumbled at the bottom of the bed. She wrote on a chart with a blue biro before returning the pen to her breast pocket and replacing the chart.

'All done for now,' she said. 'I'll leave you in peace.' Exit Nurse Minnie Mouse with a see-through envelope containing his blood.

As soon as the door closed, Trisha spoke again.

'She's left us in peace, Dad,' she said. 'Pity you never left us in peace.'

She stood up and began to pace.

'Mum was never right afterwards, you know. She tried. God help her, she tried. But she always went for the wrong men.'

Wifey was an idiot. That had become obvious over time.

He could not conceive now of any possible reason why he had ever married Wifey, but it was hardly his fault she was an idiot.

'Mum was so naïve,' his daughter continued. 'Of course, people didn't talk about things in those days.' There she was again, at the side of the bed. She leaned over and stared into his eyes. 'Can you hear me? Yes, you can, can't you? So, let's see, how many years is it since we had some quality time together? Thirty, maybe? Can you cast your mind back?'

How sarcastic she was, the little bitch.

'Of course, Mum should have faced up to things, but she didn't. You got off scot-free. You probably went on doing the same kind of thing all your life. Men like you, they don't stop, do they?'

A phone rang out, a cheerful cha cha cha tone.

'Hang on.' She reached down and he could hear a zip being unzipped, some fumbling sounds. She stood up and plonked her handbag on the bed.

'Yes, that's fine. I'll be there,' she said, into one of those new-fangled phones, before replacing it in the bag. She took out a handkerchief and blew her nose, before continuing. 'Poor Mum. I blamed her for a long time, you know. She was so naïve. In spite of those enormous blue eyes she couldn't see what was going on under her nose.'

She got up again and began to pace up and down.

'I wanted to tell her for so long, but you wouldn't let me. You said I could never tell. You used to stroke my hair. Remember? You washed my hair too. That was one of your jobs. Then you'd plait it.'

Ah yes, he had loved every hair on her little urchin head. He used to brush it for hours and smooth it into two beautiful princess-like ponytails or plait it in various delightful ways. He could almost feel the sap rising now.

How delicious it was when her little friends began to ask him to arrange their hair too; to fix it in pretty plaits like hers. Perhaps he should have been a hairdresser. In his day, only women did that job. It was a cissy job, though, and he was certainly never a cissy.

'My friends all wanted plaits like mine. Mary Kate came to our house, one day, to play. You came home early from work, remember? Mum said, "Great, you're back early. I'll just pop out to the butcher." You plaited Mary Kate's hair and then she went home and then you took down my hair and brushed it straight and you said my hair was the prettiest and that you loved me more than you loved anyone and that we had to be nice to each other. You said it was our secret. You'd have to cut my beautiful hair off if I told, and I'd have no hair left, and I'd be ugly and I'd look like a boy and that would be horrible.'

She sounded almost out of breath as she paced around the room. He couldn't see much of her but he could feel a miniscule flow of air as she moved back and forth somewhere near the foot of his bed. Maybe she was waving her arms. A windmill daughter. Or maybe a Don Quixote daughter, tilting uselessly at windmills. Once upon a time she had sat on his knee, while he read that book aloud. She was too young to understand the story, but he read it to her, anyway.

'The shock of it. I can't describe it. Seeing my friend, Mary Kate, with her hair shorn. Stubby little haircut like a boy's. The look on her face. "I'm never going to your house again," she said. "I can't be your friend anymore." I knew it was your fault, but I said nothing. You cut my hair off anyway, in the end.'

He remembered that little spoilsport, Mary Kate, who had told her mother about the fun they'd had. The little brat. She had had the most delicious chestnut hair. She told her story once, but she refused to tell it again, because he'd warned her, you see. Hair first, neck next, he'd whispered in her tiny ear. Ah, the overwhelming pleasure of that thick rope of hair shifting in his hand. Oh, the sheer joy of the blades working through the sheaf of chestnut brown. No choice but to do it once again, with his own, the blonde.

'What did you do to her? What other awful things did you do?' She leaned over him and stared right into his eyes. 'How could you live with yourself? I can hardly live with myself and I did nothing wrong. You bastard.'

She moved out of his view again and paced while she spoke.

'You know what, I was jealous. Can you believe it? You always said you loved me the most and then I found out you were doing the same things with Mary Kate. Crazy, isn't it?— but that's the way it was.'

She stopped and faced the window. Her smooth blonde hair touched the collar of her blue denim jacket. Shame it was so short, now.

'We were lucky. We got help in London,' she told the window. 'A great charity. I still donate. Only for that, we'd have been on the streets. The thing is, I've had therapy since then — loads of therapy — but I can't get over it.' She paused and took a deep breath. 'I still feel guilty,' she continued. 'We just ran away. We left you there to do as you pleased. That didn't solve anything. For men like you, there's only one solution.'

He heard her unzip her bag again. There was a metallic swishing sound.

'See what I have?' she said, towering over him now with a large chrome scissors in her hand. 'Chop chop.' She snipped the scissors open, closed, open, closed, right in front of his face.

'How do you like this?' she said. 'All these tubes. I could snip them all.'

Finally, he was afraid. It would be a painful death. Such hatred in her eyes. As usual, no Wretched Nursie, no Minnie Mousey Nursie, no little Nursie Tinybones. Like buses, there was not a single bloody Nursie around when you needed one.

He felt cold air on his lower body. She had raised the bedclothes. He could only imagine the pathetic sight; his bare old legs, the hospital nightdress, the bulge of his hospital diapers underneath. His warm urine flowed along a catheter and there was an itch somewhere on his left foot that he would never be able to scratch.

'I think I'll take your nappy off and give you a snip,' she said. 'I could do a right job on you, couldn't I? I could snip, snip, snip your dirty great thing right off.'

He felt the bedclothes being replaced carefully.

'Hmm,' she said and leaned over. She snipped the scissors several times, efficiently, in front of his face. Then she stopped and looked straight into his eyes. 'Not today,' she sighed. 'I can't be bothered today. Snip snip. I'll take my time about it. See you tomorrow.'

She picked up her handbag and held it high, so he could see her place the scissors carefully inside.

'Toodle-pip and toodle-oo,' she called, as she left the room.

Damn it, he thought, his heart racing. He had once accused Wifey of having a fancy man. He'd even tried to slap the truth out of her. He'd been certain the child was not his own. Now, he realised he had been wrong. This girl was flesh of his flesh, blood of his blood. The same feisty spirit. That zest for danger. The delicious tension. The tantalising feeling that a nurse could walk in on them at any moment. What a cunning little vixen. He was almost looking forward to her next visit.

But now the television was blank. That blasted Nurse Wretched. He wished she'd hurry up and turn it on.

MILO'S BOOK OF FEELINGS

At 6.30 a.m. Milo's mother is in the kitchen, staring at a plastic lunchbox. She's trying to think of something to put in it. This isn't easy. Milo is nine years old and he doesn't like sandwiches. Neither does he like clothes (unless they're loose, or they're hoodies with a full zip). He doesn't like loud noises, most other children, being hugged, school or homework. He hates change (unless it's an adventure). Even changing the position of the couches last week caused him anxiety. A suggestion that the bathroom should be redone caused horror. *I like it the way it is. There's nothing wrong with it.*

His lunchbox has come home from school almost untouched for the past two days and she's trying to think of something acceptable yet healthy to put in it today. She sighs.

The cats are clawing at the reinforced glass of the kitchen door, stretching and mewling for their breakfast. She gets a box of Go Cat from a cupboard and opens the door. All three kittens unbundle themselves into the kitchen with a chorus of cat complaints.

'Out,' she says and goes outside to put cat food in their plastic bowls. They follow her. The wooden decking is slick with last night's rain and feels slippery underfoot.

'Why did I ever begin to feed you lot?' she says. 'I'm a slave to you now.'

Milo's mother knows why. She found a wild but sickly young cat in the yard almost a year before. The cat was not much older than a kitten herself and it soon became clear that she was pregnant. Milo's mother bought cat food and put out milk. The kittens — three of them — were born in the old wooden shed at the bottom of the garden. Milo's mother worried and watched. Baby momma cat did her inexperienced best, but left after a few weeks, once the kittens were eating solid food. Milo's mother could hardly blame her; the kittens were a demanding bunch. They're beautiful, though, each in their own way. One is completely black, another is a tortoiseshell and the most unusual of all is an amazing smoky grey, with pale far-away eyes the colour of ashes.

Milo's mother goes inside and stares at the lunchbox again. A moment later there's a wave of wailing and meowing and scuffling noises in the backyard. She opens the door to see a big, tough-looking cat eating the kittens' food. The animal stops eating, raises his head and stares at her coldly. He has massive ears on a small head, a huge amount of orange and white fur, with a few black spots, and there's an evil look in his eyes.

'Feck off!' she says.

He doesn't move. She runs toward him and he dashes off, while she slips on the mildewed decking and falls, sliding on her hip in a graceless manner.

'Ow,' she says. She gets up and limps back to the kitchen.

She hears Milo shouting from upstairs. He's almost crying. 'Mum, where are you? Is it time to get up?'

She walks upstairs, her hand on her sore hip. 'Don't worry. Don't cry. We've plenty of time. I just had a problem outside with a cat. I'm going to call him the Evil Prince of Darkness. He was stealing the kittens' food and he made me fall over. Vile thing...'

Later that day, Milo's mother is driving him home from school.

'Why are you going out tonight, Mum?'

'I'm going to a writing class. But your Dad is coming home early. You can help him cooking dinner and you can watch a bit of TV.'

He rustles in his schoolbag. He opens the bag of Perri Popcorn she put in his lunchbox at 7 a.m. this morning. The faint smell of popcorn fills the small car.

'Mmmm, grapes. Do you want a grape, Mum?'

'No thanks. Did you eat any lunch when you were in school?'

'I didn't have enough time.'

'Why, were you playing?'

'No, I just didn't get a chance.'

Pause.

'I don't like grapes much anymore.'

'Oh. Did you like the chicken sandwich?'

'The bread was a bit strange.'

'It's pitta bread. What Arab guys eat in the desert when they get hungry and they're riding camels all day, trying to get to the next oasis.' She wonders if this is correct, but she can see the camel drivers now in her head, little rucksacks filled with school lunch boxes on their backs.

'Mum, why are you going to a writing class? I thought you could write already.'

'Well, I can read and write, that's true, but I want to write stories. It's like everything else, if you want to do something well you need to learn about it.'

'I'll help you, Mum! I have a very good imagination.'

'Oh, thanks, love. You do have a very good imagination.'

'What kind of things are you going to write?'

'God, I don't really know yet.'

Milo's mother gets to her writing class on time and spends two hours on the edge of her seat. It seems late when she gets home, though it's only nine o'clock. Her husband James has fallen asleep on the couch in front of the TV. He's a chef who works late most nights but does the lunch shift on Thursdays so she can get to her class. The supper dishes are still on the table. The remains of a chicken risotto lie congealing in a pan. She heats the food in the microwave and eats it. It's a far cry from those early days when James wooed her with his signature starter of roasted langoustines and oyster puree, with delicious lemon sole and perfect fillet steak, with the perfect Eggs Benedict he used to whip up for lazy morning breakfasts. They work so hard now and there's so little time to play, except with Milo.

An hour later, she's clearing up in the kitchen when she hears Milo upstairs, shouting and wailing in a night terror.

'No! No!' he screams. He mutters words as if possessed by the devil. It sounds as if someone is murdering him. She runs upstairs. He's already out of bed, wandering sightlessly on the landing.

He's naked because he likes to sleep 'in his nude' as he says. His long pre-teen limbs are beautiful as a young foal, but he is scared, confused, shaking in a half-world of his own fear, neither awake nor asleep.

'Now, now,' she says, leading him back to his bed. He climbs in, whimpering. 'Have a drink of water. There's nothing to worry about. Everything's fine.'

She perches at the end of the bed until he falls asleep. *Is it my fault?* she wonders. *Am I doing something wrong? Why can I not protect my beloved child from night terrors? Is there something I'm not doing... some magic chant or ritual... or merely a practical thing, such as a change of diet? Is he troubled? Surely he should not suffer torment in his sleep? Has he not got enough to deal with?*

'It never fails to scare the hell out of me,' she says to her husband, later, when she sits with him for a while. 'It's not really a nightmare, it's weird. His eyes are open but he's asleep. I don't think it's worry. I talk to him all the time. He tells me things. I think I'd know if he was upset about anything.'

'He seems happy enough.' James leans back and shoves a hand through his thick fair hair.

'I'm going to bring him to a cranial osteopath next week. That might do the trick.'

'He'll grow out of it,' says James.

Milo's mother is at the traffic lights and they've just turned green, so she needs to drive on, but she forgot to get into first gear a few seconds ago, and she's fumbling.

Milo sits in the back, talking about Runescape and what level his virtual reality alter-ego has reached. Her brain feels scrambled. A heavy-jawed taxi-driver hoots behind her and makes her jump before she sets off again.

'What does your teacher tell you to write, Mum?' he asks.

'Oh, she likes stories of love and hate and revenge... and stuff about people's deepest darkest secrets. And she likes stories where people say things but sometimes they mean something completely different. She likes figuring out what people really want, what makes them happy and what makes them sad... what secrets they have, what they're trying to hide. All kinds of things really... anything can be a story, I suppose.'

'I'll help you, Mum.'

'Great.'

Later, he hands her what looks like a piece of folded white cardboard.

'I've written a book, Mum. You can show it to your teacher if you like.'

'Gosh, this is amazing. Thank you, love.'

Some very hard work has gone into this. Her heart gladdens. He really is beginning to write, at last. It doesn't matter how bad the spelling is, so long as he's actually taking the initiative to do it. And he's organised himself to do this project. This is a huge breakthrough.

A thick decorative border, done in red marker, frames the front cover. Big curlicues of black writing spell out the words:

Milo's Book

Milo's Deepest Darkest Secrets

Keep Out!

Do not see this for your owen sake

A shaky skull and crossbones are drawn underneath.

Inside, he's glued a double page from a copybook.

There's a List of Contents on the back of the front cover.

Contents

Pg 1. Milo's heatred & love.

Pg 2. Milo's imbarising moments

Pg 3. Milo's feelings about people.

Page 1 reads:

I once was in love with Tracy but Im not any more. Below this sentence there's a shapely drawing of a heart, coloured in with red biro.

Sometimes I hate most people in the classroom. A lot of the time realy bad things happen to me.

Page 2 reads:

Once I didn't trust anyone because they were all lafing at me, and Ill never forget that.

Wen I was having my luch, wen Kelly came to my place She moct me just because I had an egg in my lunchbox.

Won time I split my hed open and I had to go to the hospital.

Page 3 reads:

Matt: a reliable friend and a good friend

Kelly: a bully

Linda: a atenchen seeker

Brian: a interesting person

Paul: a trustful friend

Jon: a energetick person and a good friend

Wen Martin is by himself he is a good laff but wen he is with Finn they are bullies.

Somtimes Joe is mean and somtimes he is OK.

Page 4 reads:

When theres niose I get realy angry

I feel bad wen people call me a loser.

I feel good wen I go to Bugger King and wen I go on adventures with my mum and dad.

I wish I was not on the spektrim.

On the back cover he has drawn a delicate yin and yang symbol, and below this are two slanted eyes, one drawn in blue biro and one in red. Lines from each eye stretch down and culminate in a multicoloured globe; he's used crayons here. The word *Dark* is written below the blue eye, the word *Light* is written underneath the red eye. There's a final sentence: *This book is about my feelings.*

Milo's mother slows down and waits to turn right. There's a lot of traffic and there's no way she can turn into the clinic unless a driver on the other side of the road stops to allow her over. A red-faced man sits in a silver Mercedes behind her. She sees his face briefly in the mirror and it feels like his stress is rolling right into her own little car. An elderly lady in a 1997 Fiat stops in the line of traffic coming in the opposite direction; she smiles and waves a hand. Milo's mother waves back and drives slowly across the road into the hospital grounds.

She parks and gets out of the car, then opens a rear door to let Milo out. He forgets to take off his seatbelt and looks confused.

'Hey,' she says. 'Seatbelt!'

He laughs as she untangles him and lifts him out.

They walk to a closed door. She's carrying his schoolbag. There's a sign saying 'Children's Unit' above the door, red letters on a white background.

'Now can you please put your hood down when you're inside? It's not noisy. You don't need your hood up all the time.'

'Do you like my book?'

'I love it. I think it's brilliant. Press the doorbell, will you, please?'

'I think I'll show it to Aoibheann.'

'Why not? I'm sure she'll like it.'

The buzzer sounds and she pushes the door open.

'Hi Sinead,' she says.

'Take a seat,' the receptionist says. 'She'll be with you in a while.'

In the waiting room, Milo's mother gets his lunchbox out

of his schoolbag and puts it on the chair next to him. She hands him a bottle of Tipperary Kidz water.

'I need my book to show Aoibheann,' he says.

'Don't you have it?' She rifles through his schoolbag but the book he made isn't there. 'Did you leave it in the car?'

'I think so.'

'OK. Stay here for a minute while I get it,' she says. 'Don't go anywhere.'

She tells the receptionist that she has to go back to the car to get something.

'No problem. Aoibheann's running a few minutes late anyway,' says Sinead.

By the time Milo's mother comes back there are crumbs all over Milo's loose clothing. An attractive woman in her late twenties enters the waiting room.

'Hello Milo. Are you ready for some fun?'

He says nothing.

'Hi, Aoibheann!' Milo's mother smiles at the occupational therapist. 'Milo, Aoibheann is talking to you.'

'Milo, are you ready?'

'Yes' he says and smiles, but he's looking at the floor, not at Aoibheann.

'Take your water in case you need it. You might get thirsty. Do you want your book?'

'Yeah.'

Milo's mother watches as he walks away with the lithe young woman. She wishes she were as lean and fit as Aoibheann. She stares at the wall blankly for a few minutes, then turns her mobile phone to silent and goes to a dark room with one-way glass. She watches the therapy session for almost an hour. Through the glass window, she sees Milo swing on a strange beanbag suspended from the ceiling and laugh with excitement and fear. He balances on a big plastic ball and grabs soft toys with his mouth, gets rolled up in a soft mat and then unrolled, lies on his stomach on a board with wheels to push himself through an obstacle course of toys and ramps, squeezes some kind of green plasticine to strengthen his hands. The occupational therapist seems to have an inexhaustible supply of energy. Milo's mother feels she could sleep for a hundred years.

She's back in the waiting room making some work calls on her mobile when Milo lopes in, followed by Aoibheann who is holding 'the book' out in front of her with a worried look.

'Can I have a word?' says Aoibheann.

Milo's mother sits in another room, one she's not been in before. There are pictures of animals on the wall and a shelf with soft toys and brightly painted wooden puzzles.

'I'm sorry to delay you,' says Aoibheann. 'but Milo showed me his book and I'm a bit concerned. I feel he may be suffering from depression. Do you think he's depressed?'

'Depressed?'

'I feel there's a lot of pain being expressed here and I wonder if you would consent to a psychological assessment? Just to be on the safe side?'

'God, I feel awful. I didn't think he was depressed at all. That thing with Kelly and the egg, that happened years ago. I mean, I know he's frustrated sometimes. But actually depressed? I don't know...'

'I'd like to organise it as soon as possible. There might even be a cancellation.'

Milo's mother gets up at 7 a.m. and feeds the triplet kittens and chases away the Evil Prince of Darkness cat (without slipping this time) and prepares a lunchbox and drives Milo to school and drives herself to her Census patch and walks miles and miles, knocking on doors that rarely open, attempting to deliver Census Forms and looks at her watch and runs to the bakery on Hope Street and drives back to the school. She parks the car illegally, since there are no spaces outside the school. She dashes in and smiles at the teacher and leads Milo out of his class as quickly as she can, and now he's in the back seat of the car with his seatbelt on.

She passes a bottle of water and a foil-wrapped package back to him, along with a couple of tissues.

'A nice warm slice of pizza.' she says. 'You can eat while we drive up there.'

They reach the clinic with five minutes to spare, and all those minutes are taken up with finding a parking space. By the time they reach the Children's Unit, Milo's mother can hardly breathe.

'Hi Sinead,' she says to the receptionist.

'She's on the phone,' says Sinead. 'But she'll be with you in a few minutes.'

In a while, the psychologist comes out, smiling. She's slim, casually dressed. She says it's nice to meet them. She stoops to talk to Milo.

'Now Milo,' says the psychologist. 'I'm going to talk with Mummy first and then you and I will have a little chat and play some games, is that all right?'

The psychologist takes Milo's mother into her office and explains the methodology she's going to use in order to ascertain Milo's state of mind. Milo's mother feels as if the conversation is floating above her head. Then the psychologist leads her back to the waiting room and takes Milo away for what seems like a long time. Milo's mother sits in the waiting room and flicks through out-of-date parenting magazines.

They come out and Milo is left to play with bright educational toys in the waiting room while his mother goes back to the psychologist's office again.

'He's fine,' the psychologist says. 'He's a lovely little boy.'

Milo's mother begins to cry. 'Sorry,' she says. 'It's just that sometimes, I'm so tired of it all.'

'You're doing a fine job,' the psychologist says. 'And it was really nice to meet you both. He's coping well, all things considered. He'll be reassessed in about six months' time, so I'll see him again then. In the meantime, if any problems come up, or you have any concerns, just ring me. Here's my card.'

'It was really nice to meet you too,' says Milo's mother. 'Though, and I hope you won't take this the wrong way, I'm sort of hoping we don't need to come and see you again for a while.'

The psychologist laughs. 'I don't blame you,' she says. She walks out with Milo's mother to the waiting room. Milo is playing Angry Birds on his mother's phone.

Milo's mother picks up Milo's bag and says, 'Time to go.'

The psychologist leads them to the door.

'Goodbye,' she says. 'It was very nice to meet you both.'

Milo nods at the floor.

Milo's mother is driving home. Her neck aches all down one side and she's feeling pre-menstrual.

'Did you have a nice time?'

'Yeah, it was okay,' says Milo. 'We were talking about feelings,'

'Was that interesting?'

'Yeah, it was alright. Then we played a few games and she gave me some stickers. Look.'

'I can't look now. I'm driving.'

'I'm really hungry.'

'I'll start cooking as soon as we get home.'

'Will we be long?'

'No. I need your help though. You need to do your homework straight away when we get home, I need to get you fed, washed and in your pyjamas before your Dad comes home so I can go out and do some work tonight.'

'Mum, did you show my book to your teacher yet?'

It begins to rain. She turns on the wipers and notices the back-windscreen wiper isn't moving. She turns the switch on and off several times, but the wiper remains stuck.

'Dammit,' she says. 'The back wiper isn't working. I hope it isn't expensive to fix. I'll have to ask your Dad.'

'So will Dad be able to fix it?'

'Remind me to ask him,' she said. 'He might. If not, I'll just have to take it to the garage.'

'Mum,' he says. He sounds happy. 'What did your teacher think of my book, Mum?'

'Well, I didn't show it to her yet. I will, when I get a chance.'

The rain is so heavy she can hear it drumming on the roof of the car, and the drops make circles on the windscreen.

'But isn't it good that I helped you, Mum? Did it help you?'

'Well, I think it's very good.' She's half-listening as she slows down and turns left into the tree-lined avenue where they live. 'I hope there's a parking space. Aha.'

She guides the car inexpertly into a space and turns off the ignition. The back-windscreen wiper is stuck at an awkward angle on the rear window. She sits there for a few seconds with her head on the steering wheel while the rain pours down.

'This is like being in the car wash,' says Milo. 'So, was my book a help, Mum? You help me, so I'll help you too.'

She sits there, not moving.

'That lady in the office said I was a great writer. And I said that was because it was in my genetic structure and I explained about chromosomes and then I told her how I think I have psychic powers and that I'm good at Art too.'

Milo's mother raises her head. 'Yes, she told me she really enjoyed her chat with you. She said she hasn't had so much fun in ages.'

The rain eases off and she gets out of the car and opens the back door to let Milo out. As usual, he tries to get out of the car with his seatbelt on.

'Seatbelt,' she says and then regrets the sharpness of her voice.

She opens the gate to their house. The sky is clearing now. In the small front yard the dustbin has overturned, and wet litter is strewn all over the ground. Milo's mother sighs and looks at the mess. Then she hears a scuffling noise. She glances around, searching for its source. A yellow Maynard Wine Gum bag with a fluffy body attached to it moves amid the litter. It's a cat. He's got his head stuck inside the bag and his ears are preventing the bag from falling off. The cat walks around in circles until he bumps into the wall. Milo's mother begins to laugh.

'Look Milo,' she says. 'It's the cat I call the Evil Prince of Darkness. He's been trapped by his own greed!'

'Will we help him, Mum?' says Milo worriedly, keeping his distance.

'Yes, I'll sort him out in a minute. Hey, I'll take a photo of him first. No, you take the photo, you're much better.'

She gives him her mobile phone and he smiles, then takes two photographs.

'Well done,' says his mother. 'Brilliant! You've got such a

good eye.'

She puts her arms out wide around him without touching his body. She knows better than to hold him close. She kisses the side of his hoodie. Very gently so he can't feel it.

'Thank you,' she says. 'I don't know what I'd do without you.'

She unlocks the front door. Milo walks in, then turns. 'So, what's your story about, Mum?'

She pauses, then says, 'Love, I think... Yes, it's mostly a story about love.'

DIGNITY

On the Friday when all the trouble began — though I didn't know that until some days later — my sister Ellie arrived at my house at 7 a.m. as usual. She took the black plastic folder out of her massive handbag — I call it her Mary Poppins bag because you never know what she'll take out of it next — and put it on my bedside cabinet.

'I think it's best to keep it here,' she said. 'And Jake might want to check it out when he comes on Sunday.'

Jake's my son. He's working in Dublin now but he often comes down at weekends.

'Now, let's get you sorted,' she said.

'Absolutely,' I agreed. 'Let's get out of here before Mrs. Looney arrives.'

Mrs. Looney cleans my house on Friday mornings. I like to be out when she's in. Bad enough that Mrs. Looney has an irritating way of telling me to count my blessings and believe in the power of prayer; but she never stops complaining herself, about her arthritis, her bunions and her old blaggard of a husband. In fact, if you listened to her and you didn't know better, you'd swear that Mrs. Looney was the one in constant agony and that there was nothing much wrong with me. I used to do an impression of the auld bag that made Ellie hoot with laughter, but the joke has worn thin at this stage.

So that's why Ellie usually takes me shopping on Fridays. We often go to Leevale Shopping City. You can find some decent stuff in the shops there, and the supermarket has nice wide aisles.

There are two disabled parking spaces right near the main entrance of Leevale Shopping City and that's where we prefer to park, especially since I got the Power Chair. There's usually only one space free and sometimes none; I'd been ranting about it for ages because every time we went to Leevale, no matter what time we arrived, the same creamy white Fiat 500 with a red interior was parked neatly in one of our disabled spaces.

Rain was pouring from the heavens as we arrived, to see the white Fiat sliding into our parking spot. A young woman in a smart raincoat got out of the Fiat and clicked the car locked before trotting into the shopping centre—not a bother on her despite the high heels—which were gorgeous by the way, possibly Kurt Geiger; I used to have a pair like them.

'The cheek of her,' said Ellie, as she opened the back of the Renault and got out the wheelchair ramp.

'Let's follow her,' I said, but by the time I'd manoeuvred my Power Chair down the ramp and motored into the shopping centre she was nowhere to be seen. We went into Boots the Chemist first, to get my prescriptions, and while we were there, Ellie got the notion to ask the pharmacist if she knew the woman who drove the Fiat.

'That one? She owns the Happy Hair salon.'

'Is she disabled?'

'No.'

'Well, do you know what? She always parks in that disabled space right outside the main door,' Ellie said and the girl said that would be her alright, and wrinkled up her face and raised her eyebrows in a manner that meant, quite unmistakably, that she couldn't stand the woman.

I wasn't much in the mood for shopping, so we didn't stay long. Outside, the rain had stopped and the white Fiat was still in the same spot.

'What a complete bitch,' Ellie said.

'We should do something about it,' I said. 'You could let the air out of her tyres.'

'I could. But should I?'

'Do,' said I. 'And we'll leave her a note.'

'Brilliant,' said Ellie. 'What will we write?'

'How about "WHO'S DISABLED NOW?"' I said.

Ellie nearly exploded with laughter. This is one of the many reasons I love my sister; she's so steady and reliable most of the time, but when she gets all fired up she turns into a rebel.

'Hurry,' I said.

She kept glancing around like a fugitive while she let the air out of both rear tyres. Then she tore the blank bit off our shopping list and scrawled the words on it and added three big exclamation marks and tucked it behind the Fiat's windscreen wipers before we made our getaway.

As Ellie revved up and drove off she was laughing fit to burst. I started too, but in a few seconds I was laughing so hard I started choking. Sometimes this happens when my saliva goes down the wrong way. She had to pull up around the corner and hop out to sort me out. She reached in to pat me on the back and hold my head for a minute until I could breathe again and said, 'Easy now, easy does it.' She got a tissue out of her pocket and wiped the dribble off my chin.

'You gave me a fright there,' she said.

Then we started laughing again, this time I didn't choke and for a while I felt almost human again because there's nothing like a good laugh, even in the worst of times.

By the time we got back to my house, Mrs. Looney had been and gone. The floor was still wet, so at least she'd pushed the goddam mop around. It should be easy enough to clean the place. Even now, every time I come home I forget, just for a second or two, that the house is no longer how it used to be. A few years back, Jake insisted on getting the ground floor renovated, though I told him repeatedly that I didn't intend to hang round long enough to make all that trouble and expense worthwhile. Jake was always great at organising things, even as a kid. He called in favours, got an architect friend to draw up the plans for free, did some deals and pulled it all together like that DIY SOS programme on the BBC and all I gave him at the time was grief because I had to go to a Respite Care Home while the builders were in and I hated it there. I felt mean about it afterwards and I apologised, because the new downstairs meant that I didn't always need a carer around, until recently. I've almost forgotten what the upstairs rooms look like; they might as well be distant planets now.

It's frustrating not to be able to take care of things myself. Ellie does a lot. She does more housework than Mrs. Looney for sure, and, on top of that, she's now my carer as well, but the pay doesn't cover anything like the time she puts in. Sometimes I get all bitter and twisted thinking about how much she has to do.

That day, though, it seemed as if Mrs. Looney had done a half-decent job until we went into the kitchen area, where she'd left the top bits from the hob still soaking in the sink. Ellie sighed, then bent down and opened the oven door. She stared in.

'She never cleaned the bloody oven. I specifically asked her. She's hopeless. Absolutely hopeless. We'll have to get rid of her and get someone else.'

'It's hardly worth it, for the sake of a few months,' I slurred. My speech is getting very bad.

'Oh God,' she said. 'It sounds terrible when you say it like that.'

'Sorry.'

'It's not your fault.' She came over and hugged me. Then she looked me in the eyes. 'You're going to tell Jake on Sunday, aren't you? You have to. I'm not going to do it.'

'Yeah, 'course I will.'

'He'll be upset.'

'I know.'

Even now, stuck in my so-called Power Chair, I love to watch the Grand Prix on TV. I've always loved cars. Dad was a mechanic, and our mother died young, so Ellie and I spent many hours hanging around his garage in Ballyphehane. Friday nights were best, when we'd sit in the back seat of whatever car Dad was working on, eating battered cod and vinegary chips from Lennox's, the fried smell melding with the fumes of engine oil. He'd eat much faster than we did so he could get back to tinkering underneath a bonnet, persuading an engine to roar back to life, before wiping his greasy hands on his overalls and declaring that it was time to quit.

I must have seemed a strange little girl. Ellie liked dolls but I far preferred cars. I could drive by the time I was ten and for my seventeenth birthday Dad bought me a bright red

Triumph Herald. It was second-hand, of course — 1965 — and it needed a bit of work, but I loved it. Even now, although I like perfume well enough, my favourite scent is petrol.

It was Formula One season again and I was looking forward to watching the Belgian Grand Prix at the weekend. The noise of roaring revving engines and the sight of crazily fast cars zipping around a racing track raises my spirits and comforts me, even on bad days when my bones poke against my flesh like shards of ice and I have to grind my teeth together to stop myself groaning.

Jake arrived on Sunday, at about 3 p.m. He hugged me gently; he knows by now that big hugs are painful.

'You're looking well,' I told him.

'Thanks,' he said. 'You're not looking too bad yourself, all things considered.'

That made me laugh, in spite of myself.

While Ellie made stuffing for the chicken and prepared a trifle, Jake replaced a bulb in the bathroom and put a new washer on the kitchen tap. All I could do was sit there like a spare part, watching them work.

When it was almost 5 p.m., Ellie got me sorted, toilet-wise, and settled me back in the Power Chair while Jake went out for a cigarette. Then we sat round the television, glued to Sky Sports. For a while I was engrossed in the bustling activity of the mechanics in the paddock, while commentators tried to catch a final few words with drivers and team bosses and the occasional celebrity before the race began. Finally the cars were in position and the red lights turned to green and I could almost smell the petrol and exhaust fumes and every time they showed the camera angle from Lewis Hamilton's car, it was almost as if I was behind the wheel myself, surging ahead, arcing around the chicanes, slowing into the pit lane when his team manager said 'box, box, box,' and zipping relentlessly into the lead again, and I could almost forget the bones that pinned every part of me down in pain.

Rosberg won and Lewis Hamilton only came third, for a change, but considering Lewis started from the back row on the grid he did brilliantly. Daniel Ricciardo came second and I was thrilled because he hasn't the best car so he doesn't often get placed. To be honest, I've a soft spot for Danny Ric; I love his toothy smile. All in all, it was a fine race and afterwards I figured it was time for a drink before dinner.

'Can I do anything?' Jake asked his aunt Ellie. In fairness, he has lovely manners; I've always been determined that he wouldn't turn out like his father.

'No, the chicken's in,' Ellie told him. 'And everything else is prepped.' She took her apron off and hung it over one of the kitchen chairs, then ran her fingers through her hair. She looked at her watch. 'I have to collect Jim and bring him over. I won't be long. In the meantime, you might as well start on the wine. There's plenty in the fridge.'

Her face was a little flushed. Ellie has always been as transparent as glass. My brother-in-law Jim is the solid, reliable kind. If he's supposed to turn up for his dinner at seven, he'll be there at seven. Besides, they only live ten minutes away. When I looked at Jake I knew he was thinking the same thing.

As the front door banged shut, Jake moved to the fridge and took out a bottle of Albarino. He poured some into my pink plastic mug and clicked the safety top on before he handed it to me.

'Baby cup. I hate it,' I said, and my hands shook terribly as I held it. I knew Jake was wondering whether or not to offer help, but all he said was 'I know,' as he poured a glass of wine for himself.

'So, what's up with Aunt Ellie?' he said then.

'You won't like it.' My speech was very slurred. I hate that. At first it happened when I was tired or stressed, but now it's just another part of the damaged package that is me.

'No matter. Fire away.'

'I made a decision, Jake.'

'Go on.'

'Well, the date is set. I'm going to Dignitas at the end of November. After the final Grand Prix.'

'But, that's only — is it — ten weeks away? Mam, you can't.'

'Look Jake, I've held out for thirteen years but it's too hard. I can't face another Christmas.'

'It's just... I know you've talked about it before, but over there in Dignitas... it looks like a factory building. I mean, I'm sure it's fine inside, but... wouldn't you prefer to die here at home?'

'I would, but sure it's illegal here. What choice do I have?'

Jake chewed the inside of his lip, then slugged back all the wine in his glass.

'Would you think about leaving it a while longer?'

'I can't, Jake. If I wait too long I might be too banjaxed to travel and then I'll be stuck.'

'It's not right Mam. It's much too soon.' He shifted in his chair and bit his lip again. Then he raised his head and stared through the kitchen window. I moved my head with difficulty so that I could see what he was looking at. Out in the yard, a robin redbreast perched on a limb of the rotary washing line.

'That little robin turns up every day,' I said. 'Ellie feeds him for me now.'

'I'm going out for a cigarette,' he said.

'You'll kill yourself with them fags.'

'Look who's talking.' He shook his head and went out into the backyard. If I could have swallowed my stupid words I would have. As I sat powerless in my Power Chair I could see him pacing in the dusk, dragging on his cigarette as if it was a punishment.

When Jake came back in, I could smell the fags off him. I worried that in some small ways he'd taken after his father. When I was young, Lorcan Hickey's edginess and fast talk had fascinated me, but he had turned out to be a flawed and faithless man. He cheated on me when I was pregnant, so I left him and came home. Ellie and Jim helped me then too. I could never have managed on my own.

Jake tilted the bottle of wine towards my plastic cup and I shook my head. Then he poured more wine into his glass.

'It's beginning to get cloudy,' he said. 'There'll be no stars tonight.'

'You had a telescope when you were twelve. Do you remember?'

He half-smiled. 'That was such a good present. I still love all that stuff, which reminds me, did you know that NASA has discovered a new planet? Kepler 452b. They're calling it Earth 2.0 because it's the closest match yet to our own planet.'

He got his iPad out and found a YouTube clip. The planet floated pale in an inky black universe, circling a sun-like star. Its pocked surface looked a lot like Earth.

'Maybe there's a whole other race up there,' he said.

'I hope it's an improvement on the crowd down here anyway.'

I liked the thought of Earth 2.0. I never tell other people what to believe and I don't believe in anything much myself, except that if there's a God I'm quite happy to meet her and explain myself. I like the idea of God being a woman, though of course if there is a God at all, it might be anything, half and half for all I know, or just a cloud that talks or sends telepathic messages. Or there might be nothing. But if there's nothing, then there's nothing. I'll be dead and I won't even know there's nothing anyway and there's no way I can change that.

'Replay it for me,' I said. I wanted to see Earth 2.0 again. Jake pressed the tab and we stared at the screen.

'So you're not going to change your mind?"

'No.'

'Who's taking you there?'

'Ellie. Jim's coming too. All the details are in a black folder in my bedroom.'

'I'll go as well.'

'Jake, there's no need. The less people involved, the better.'

'Ah Mam,' he said. He slugged back more wine. Then he got up and hugged me very gently.

'You can't come with me,' I said, into his chest. 'I already decided that. You have your career to think about — your whole life is in front of you.'

'Look, it's about time I copped onto myself. I could fly from Dublin and meet you in Zurich. Where's that folder?' He found it and slapped it down on the kitchen table. 'Right,' he said. 'I'll book my flights this minute,' but he didn't open the folder. Instead he sat there, and I expected him to protest again, but then I saw tears in his eyes, and all of a sudden he looked about five years old again. I felt my own face getting wet in spite of myself. He found a box of tissues and wiped my eyes, and then his own.

The MS was diagnosed thirteen years ago, when I was forty-five. It's the worst kind, and the truth is that I'm slowly and painfully dying with no prospect of even a brief remission. After I got the diagnosis, I kept on working and driving as long as I could, even when I finally had to use a walking stick. In fairness, even then I managed okay until I had an unfortunate accident on Pouladuff

Road — involving a muscle spasm in my right leg and a lot of damage to the back of poor old Mr. Dearborne's car — and realised my driving days were over. I had to quit work in the University soon afterwards but at least I had a good pension plan. It nearly broke my heart to sell my little Audi TT but Jim found me a Renault with disabled access for a wheelchair so that he or Ellie could take me out.

The crunch came in the early hours after a terrible night when I lay awake, crying. My drug regime was causing complications almost as bad as the condition and my stomach was giving me grief. On top of that I had pruritis again and the itching was excruciating; enough to drive a person crazy. My bones ached as if I was being pulled on a rack and my head was so sensitive that it felt as if the roots of my hair were digging into my brain. I'm not one for moaning all the time but I was in agony. Jesus Christ, I moaned. Fucking hell. Christ Almighty. Oh God, oh God, oh God help me. It's amazing that all my groaning was to a God I didn't believe in. No God of any kind of quality could ever have wished this on me. I knew no sleep would come, but at about five in the morning, with much difficulty I managed to pull myself up and across into the Power Chair and I trundled into the main room.

To distract myself until Ellie arrived, I decided to watch a documentary about Senna again. He was an amazing talent, who sadly crashed and died at the San Marino Grand Prix in 1994. He was only thirty-four, same age as my son Jake is now. Senna prayed to God before the race, but God didn't save him. That's the way of it. No wonder I'm not impressed with God. Bad things can happen to anybody.

The DVD was easy to spot, not too high up on the shelves, with 'SENNA' written in yellow capital letters on the spine. I raised my hand as best I could and reached for it. Almost there, I leaned out of the flipping Power Chair but my right leg went into spasm and I tipped sideways, slithering right off the wheelchair hard onto the floor. That was that. No way could I get up.

As I lay there, my hips and shoulders felt like razorblades and I couldn't help scraping at my itching parts, all the while knowing that this would only make the problem worse. Under the TV stand, a spider's web was flecked with desicated fly corpses, crumbs and other debris... the white... not maggots, surely not? Why hadn't that bitch Looney bothered to hoover underneath? The stand was on wheels, for feck sake.

The clock on the mantelpiece ticked a familiar clicking sound. It seemed to get louder and louder and the sound of it annoyed the hell out of me. My panic alarm was miles away on my bedside cabinet (Ellie's always at me to keep it round my neck) so I tried to drag myself back into the bedroom but I was like a slug on salt, pierced with pain and getting colder and colder. By the time Ellie arrived, on the dot of seven, all I could say was 'Ellie, it's time.'

On the Monday after our Friday escapade at Leevale Shopping City, Jake left for Dublin at the crack of dawn and Ellie came in as usual at 7 a.m. I was in a lot of pain that day and I didn't want to go anywhere. I listened to BBC Radio One Extra and asked Ellie to give me extra pain relief. Before Ellie went home for an hour in the afternoon, she put a recording of the July Grand Prix for me— the British one, at Silverstone. It was an exciting race and I wanted to watch it again even though I already knew Lewis had won.

When the front door buzzer rang, I wondered who on earth it could be. Jake was back in Dublin as far as I knew. Ellie, Jim and Mrs. Looney had keys. Not many other people came round anymore. I can't really blame them. Most people, when faced with someone who has an incurable disease, don't know what to say, so they stay away instead.

I fumbled for the remote control to pause the recording but it wasn't in my 'Super Storage System'. The Super Storage System, as I call it, is a pocketed thing made of grey fleece fabric and held firmly by a Velcro fastening onto one side of the Power Chair. Ellie got it for me so that I could bung things in that I'd need when I was alone, like the TV remote, the DVD remote, my reading glasses, water bottle, tissues and phone, but the trouble is I keep so many things in there now I can hardly find anything right off.

It was a few seconds before I realised the remote was on the small table beside me all the while. I pressed the wrong button first and the race zoomed forward instead of pausing. By the time I managed to pause the flipping recording the front door buzzer had stopped, but then it buzzed again and, thankfully, the intercom thingy was in its rightful place in the Super Storage System so I managed to get it out and press the Talk button.

'Who's there?' I asked.

'It's the police.' The man's voice sounded tinny and officious through the intercom. 'Sorry to disturb you but we need to ask a few questions.'

It was ludicrous, I realised, afterwards, but the first thing that came to mind was that myself and Ellie were in trouble over what we'd done on Friday to the Fiat belonging to the Happy Hair girl in Leevale Shopping Centre.

I zoomed too fast into the hall, bumping my wheelchair against the doorframe and cursing under my breath. Then I hesitated for a moment. Sometimes this blinking MS makes my head addled, so I tried to force myself to think clearly. I'd admit nothing but I'd point out that if a young woman in the full bloom of her health was mean enough to park in a disabled parking space, she deserved what she got. I spoke through the intercom.

'Show some ID,' I said.

I peered through the spyhole, which Jake, bless him, had made sure to place low in the door, and then I pressed the Open button and invited them in.

Two Gardaí stepped into the hall. The man, a tall thin fellow in uniform, had hardly any chin. He was what my Dad used to call 'a chinless wonder'. The female Garda was fair-haired and looked no more than sixteen, in spite of the fact that she wore an engagement ring and a wedding band. Her perfume smelt of woods and flowers; it was probably Issey Miyake

The Garda looked down at me past his almost non-existent chin. 'Is your name Mrs. Siofra O'Sullivan?' he asked, very slowly.

'Mizz. Is there a problem?' My words came out a bit blubbery and I felt spit seeping onto my lower lip. It always gets worse when I'm anxious.

'I'm sorry for the intrusion,' said the female cop. 'We just want to ask you a few questions.'

'You might as well come in,' I said. Without waiting for them, I reversed backwards and then drove left through the door that led into the living area. I bumped into the table as I turned the wheelchair round to face them.

'I wish they didn't call it a Power Chair,' I said. 'This damn thing is more like a bumper car.'

The female officer nodded and the chinless wonder didn't seem to notice that I'd spoken.

'Can you tell me the nature of your disability?' he said slowly, pronouncing each word as if he were speaking to a child.

'There's no need to talk like that,' I slurred. 'I'm no Stephen Hawking but I'm not a vegetable either.'

'I'm sorry,' said the female cop. 'Today's one of his slow

days.'

'Sorry,' he blushed.

'It's okay,' I said. 'I'm used to it. Primary Progressive Multiple Sclerosis is what I've got.'

'It must be tough,' the girl said.

'It is. There's no cure and in my case there's no remission. Would you like to sit down, while you're here?'

They placed themselves awkwardly on the couch.

'Is Ellie O'Sullivan Gould your sister?' the chinless wonder asked, this time in a normal voice.

'Yes. And she's my carer as well.'

'There's been a report that she's taking you to Switzerland. To Dignitas.'

'What... who told you that?' I felt stricken. A line from a poem came daftly into my head. *The best laid plans of mice and men...*

'Assisting a suicide is a criminal offence under section 2 of the Criminal Justice (Suicide) Act 1993, so we're obliged to investigate.'

'No one is assisting me to do anything. I can't go anywhere on my own. I always need someone to travel with me.'

'I'm terrible sorry, Mrs. O'Sullivan,' he said, and he did seem sorry, in fairness. 'I don't want to alarm you but there's a possibility that your sister will be charged if she brings you to Dignitas,' he said.

'But it's in a different country. It's legal there.'

'Unfortunately, the law in this country hasn't changed, Mrs. O'Sullivan ...'

'It's "Mizz", I said. 'And I won't answer any more questions without a solicitor present.'

'Sorry. Make a note of that,' he told the girl cop. She didn't look at him and she didn't look at me either. She just stared at whatever she'd written in her notebook.

'We're very sorry to bother you,' he said. 'I hope we don't have to follow this up but we'll have to file a preliminary report before we know any more.'

'We'll let ourselves out,' the girl said, and they got up and left.

I could hardly believe it. I was raging. So much planning. The agony of filling out forms and getting up-to-date medical reports and psychological reports. I'd had my will drawn up and witnessed. I'd bought Christmas presents to be unwrapped after I was dead. A special parcel for Jake on his wedding day if he ever got married — I hoped he'd tie the knot with Donna... The waiting... Four months it took to get Dignitas sorted and I had only six months to take up the place or I'd have to update the blasted reports and start all over again.

On the TV screen, the front of Lewis Hamilton's silver Mercedes was freeze-framed on the silent racing track. I stared at the back of his white helmet and his white-gloved hands on the steering wheel as he sat there, going nowhere.

Then the doorbell rang again.

It was the girl cop's voice on the intercom this time.

'Sorry, I left my notebook behind.'

'Ah feck off,' I muttered but all the same I pressed Open. The girl came in. Her face was flushed.

'Actually, I didn't leave anything behind,' she said. 'I've come back to apologise. I'm really, really sorry. Sometimes I hate my job.'

She left before I could think of anything to say, and, mercifully, before I soiled my incontinence pad. I sat in despair for some moments, before driving myself into the bathroom. Exhausted at the thought of the slow unsavoury cleansing that lay ahead, I couldn't help breaking down in tears. That's how Ellie found me when she arrived a few minutes later.

'We're busted, Ellie,' I wailed. 'And I've shat myself.'

'I know,' said Ellie. 'Don't worry about that now. Let's get you sorted.'

Ellie helped me undress and sit in the shower. She washed and dried me and helped me put my nightclothes on. She poured a glass of the good brandy and folded my hand around it.

'The police just called me. That's why I'm late.'

'How did they find out?' I slurred. 'I bet it was that old wagon Mrs. Looney. Always banging on about prayer and offering it up...'

'I brought the folder over here last Friday,' said Ellie. 'I shouldn't have done that.'

Given that my law-abiding brother-in-law Jim has never even been done for speeding, his attempts to keep us all calm and pretend he wasn't worried were almost convincing.

'It'll all work out in the mix,' he said. Jim used to be a sound engineer, back in the day. 'Don't worry about it.'

Ellie wasn't calm at all. She phoned her solicitor and hounded him for information on possible outcomes and worst-case scenarios. Jake's name didn't come up at all, which was the only scrap of comfort for me.

Finally, weeks later, the police heard back from the Director of Public Prosecutions. No charges would be made. There was 'no realistic prospect of conviction'.

'Side-stepping the issue,' grumbled Jim. 'But at least that's that, for now.'

'You'll just have to plough on a while longer,' Ellie said

to me. 'We'll have to leave it for now. I'm glad you're still here, to be honest.'

'I'm stuck, Ellie.'

'No, you're not. We'll sort something out. You'll see.'

I nodded, but I knew in my heart I couldn't put them through all that again.

The final Grand Prix was on Sunday 27th November. Jake came down from Dublin again, to watch it with me. I tried not to show how grim I felt. I took more pain relief than usual. Hamilton won and Rosberg came in second. Jim arrived afterwards. We ate a very fine beef stew and drank champagne and I talked a lot and told them I loved them, and they thought it was because I was drunk, and I was, but it wasn't, and it was a great day but that night I hardly slept at all and I woke in the early hours with a horrid sensation of internal shakiness and my whole being in endless pain.

The package didn't arrive on Monday. It was supposed to arrive for definite that week, so I'd struggled to get up by myself at 7 a.m. It took ages to put my dressing jacket on, and my pad was soggy. It was taking me longer to manoeuvre myself into the Power Chair, but I was not completely incapable yet.

The last thing I wanted was for the postman to rush off without delivering the package and leave one of those notes telling me to collect it at the sorting office. If I missed the delivery, the sorting office was way out beyond the Kinsale Roundabout and I'd have to ask Ellie or Jim to collect it. But I was determined that no one would know about the package or find out what was inside. I'd pleaded with Ellie to stay home until noon all this week. I claimed I was sleeping better, later, in the mornings, that I needed time alone.

By 7 a.m. on Tuesday I was struggling to ready myself once more. When the doorbell finally rang, just after nine, I was terrified I wouldn't reach the front door on time, but I made it. Alan, the postman, was outside, holding a package. The stamps looked foreign. When he asked me to sign for it my hands were so unwieldy that all I could manage was an illegible scrawl. He handed the package to me but I lost my grip and it fell to the ground.

'I'll bring it inside for you, will I?' he asked. He came in and put it down on the kitchen table. 'You want me to open it for you, love?'

'No thanks, Alan. I'm fine now,' I said.

It was difficult, but I managed to slice at the sellotape gently with a serrated knife for ages until the end of the package came loose — scissors were way too difficult. Then I tore slowly at the cardboard until the contents were revealed.

It was a shock to see a shiny purple box with the words *Catch Me... Cacharel* written in white, below a cluster of circles in pink, white and puce. It seemed to be perfume or body lotion. How could this be? I'm such an ejit, I thought. The one thing I'd not imagined was that I'd be conned.

It hadn't been easy sending $450 to the company in Mexico; hours of pecking away at my computer, making mistakes, fumbling and foosthering during the increasingly rare times I spent alone.

But maybe, just maybe... I tried to open the perfume box. Feck. Tore it. But... oh joy. Inside, two glorious bottles of Nembutal. 200 ml in clear liquid form. Now to manage pouring a cup of the good brandy — to wash it down. That worked well, according to the blogs. I'd done my research.

But then I was afraid. I didn't want to die in secrecy. I knew exactly what I wanted. *To cease upon the midnight with no pain.* A calm, quiet letting go, with my loved ones around me. But here I was, terribly alone.

I tried to think about Earth 2.0 and what it might be like there, but no matter how I tried, I couldn't picture it.

THE SILENCE OF THE CROWS

O nce again, I woke up at 5 a.m. to the sound of those damn crows scratching and scrabbling in the attic space above my head. Every morning for weeks now, the pair of them had been cawing and squawking in the early hours, fussing and flapping under the eaves, making scraping sounds across the ceiling, building and rebuilding their flipping nest under our roof. Sometimes they sounded as if they were moving furniture around up there. I would never have believed that crows could make such a racket, had I not been forced to listen.

At first, I'd almost admired those crows. I still had a sneaking respect for them, because they worked so hard, obviously determined to create the ideal nest. I remembered how James and I had fussed and fretted before Milo was born. Everything had to be as perfect as it could be: the Moses basket, the tiny hypoallergenic mattress, the soft cellular cotton baby blankets, the wooden cot, the decorative border with sweet cartoon animals on the nursery walls.

Our lovely house was more than a hundred years old and

I'd longed for it as soon as I saw it. The surveyor had warned us at the time about the state of the roof but we were in a mad rush because we'd sold our place in Dublin and were squandering money on rent in Cork, plus Milo was due in three months. Now, nine years later, we had a serious hole in the roof and a pair of crows were living, rent-free and raucous, in the attic. I needed my sleep and those crows had to go.

James didn't care so much about the roof problem. He thought the whole thing could be solved by replacing a few slates, like we'd done a few years' back. He's a chef and mostly works on late shifts, so he'd taken to sleeping on a bed settee in the box room on the floor below. Milo's room was on that floor too, so he didn't hear the squawking either. Just as well, for he needed plenty of sleep to cope with the demands of school.

I tried to ignore the sound of the crows but it was impossible. I got up and flung the dormer window open. I banged a wooden coat hanger against the roof tiles, and the crows cawed viciously and shot out of the hole in the roof above me. But by now I knew that this was only a temporary departure.

Mr. Crow, his jet-black feathers gleaming, was the size of a small dog. As usual on these occasions, he perched on top of the lamppost outside the house and glared through the window at me with his beady eyes. Mrs. Crow (or so I presumed, as she was slightly smaller) placed herself farther away on one of the sycamore trees on the other side of the street and cursed me under her beaky breath. I knew those crows recognised me and hated me.

'I'm not going to be bullied by two members of the Corvid family,' I told them. 'I have my own small family to consider.'

Then I shut the window firmly and went back to bed. I

covered my head with the duvet but it was hopeless. James had banged the front door closed when he arrived home at 2 a.m. A couple of hours later, the crows had murdered what little sleep remained. There was nothing for it but to get up.

I crept down the first set of stairs and stopped on the landing. The door of the box-room was open and James was submerged under a duvet, his mane of straw-yellow hair the only part of him visible. His filthy chef's whites rose up from the floor in a stinking heap. I picked them up as usual and brought them downstairs to soak them in OxyClean.

After I had a shower and got dressed, I fed the feral cats who were clawing at the back door, rinsed the whites and shoved them in the washing machine, got Milo's lunchbox ready and woke him up to have his breakfast before it was time to leave for school.

The crows had deliberately targeted my car again. Random splats of grey-white bird poop dotted the roof and the front windscreen. I was convinced they knew what I was planning, that they chose my car, not because it's red, but because I was the enemy. Most days there was bird shit on my car, but the vehicles parked on either side were spared.

'They've done it again, Mum!' Milo said. The vindictiveness of our crows never failed to entertain him.

'Fuck it,' I said.

'You're always saying I shouldn't curse,' said Milo.

I buckled him into the back seat and sat behind the wheel. I turned the wipers on to wash the remains of the bird shit off my windscreen. I watched the water dribble weakly, and then run out, leaving a disgusting greyish smear across the glass. I badly wanted to curse again.

'Crows are very intelligent,' Milo said. 'They can remember people, just like elephants.'

'Stay there and don't you dare budge,' I told him. I dashed back to the house, filled a watering can and raced outside again. I raised the bonnet of the car and filled the water tank. When I got back in the car, I tossed the watering can in the footwell and turned on the ignition. I turned the wipers on full blast and the water sprayed across the windscreen, frantically beating back and forth until the worst of the grey-white shite was gone.

'I hate those crows,' I said as I put the car into gear.

'You shouldn't hate anything,' Milo said, sanctimoniously, from the back seat. 'Hate is the same as Wrath, and Wrath is one of the seven deadly sins.'

'Right. I dislike the crows intensely.'

'There's six more deadly sins,' Milo said. 'Greed, sloth, gluttony, pride, lust and envy.'

'Impressive,' I said. It's amazing the things that he retains—and the things he can't remember. He's not exactly your average child but he's all the more loveable because of that. James and I adore him. When he was born, we decided those early years were so important that we'd never both work full-time while he was young. Which turned out to be me working freelance as a technical editor plus doing everything else on the home front—losing my place on the career ladder and most of my earning power—but Milo, my beautiful flaxen-haired smiling boy, made up for everything.

The new roof was going to cost a fortune—the bones of €20,000—but I was determined to get it done before the winter. Unbeknownst to James, I'd been saving up for a new roof for years but I was still a few grand short. James was furious when he found out about my nest egg, but I forced him to admit that if he'd known about the money, we wouldn't have it.

I'd taken a part-time, temporary job with the CSO, as a Census Enumerator, figuring I could fit it in easily around Milo's schedule and my freelance work. The extra three grand would be just enough, on top of my savings, to get the roof done. A proper job. The right slates, that would look exactly like the originals. Plenty of insulation underneath the eaves; we'd face much lower heating bills next winter. A new dormer window, with a wooden surround and a replacement finial on top. The builder knew a wood-turner who would make one exactly like the original.

I'd already handed over a deposit. The builder, Donal, would put the scaffolding up in July, he said. It wouldn't take too long, he said. I mentioned the crows' nest in case it proved to be a problem. He said he had previous experience of crows. They can be vicious, he said, especially when you're dealing with them at that height, but you've just got to learn how to protect yourself from them. Donal was bald and brawny. We'd grown up together on the same estate in Ballincollig. Donal and his crew were more than a match for my crows, he assured me, and I believed him.

After I delivered Milo to school, I drove to my Census patch and parked near the Hot Stuff Café on Hope Street. I put on the ugly jacket and the yellow Hi Viz waistcoat that my Supervisor insisted was obligatory and hung the lanyard with my ID Badge round my neck. Even though I'd only been working on the Census for a few days, I was already sick and tired of knocking on strangers' doors.

It was one of those part-time jobs that seemed so easy and convenient in the advertisement but was a nightmare in reality. Delivering Census forms was like playing slot machines or herding cats. Some people were at home in the morning, some in the afternoon, some in the evening when I couldn't go out unless James had a night off to take care of Milo. Some people never seemed to be home, or if they were, they weren't answering their doors. It didn't help that the stupid Hi Viz jacket made me look like I was collecting for a charity.

If it was just a case of shoving a Census Form through every letterbox the job wouldn't have been so bad. But posting a form through the letterbox was a last resort, only permitted after four or five attempts to make contact with the householder. The training had been very clear on this. Doing the first part of the work properly — delivering the forms — would make things much easier later on, my Supervisor had insisted.

After Census Day, I'd have to go back to every house again to collect the completed form. The thought of doing it all over again made me sick to my stomach, but I'd never been a quitter. I'd had to give up going to my writing class, but I told myself I'd find time for it again, maybe in the autumn. I forced myself to think about the new roof, the silence of the crows, the beautiful wood-turned finial that would perch atop the wooden surround of my new dormer window and look exactly like the original. I checked the horrid bag to make sure I had my clipboard, a pen, my Record Book, my neatly folded map, enough forms and calling cards for a couple of hours work, slipped the antiquated mobile phone I'd been supplied with into a pocket and hauled myself out of the car. Off I went, on yet another thankless round of ringing doorbells and knocking on doors, hoping for a decent day.

The weather had been like a lucky dip since I started the job but at least it wasn't raining. That day, I began my route in Liberty Terrace, a row of small redbrick houses off Hope Street. It was a pleasant little square, with a small green park opposite the houses, and beyond it the back walls of another row of houses and bordered by Hope Street on one side and two other, larger, detached houses on the other.

A dapper elderly gentleman called Declan O'Toole answered the door of Number 2. A retired Chief Superintendent in the police, he cheered me up considerably.

'I know nearly everyone around here,' he said. 'Come back to me if you have any problems, or if you'd like a cup of tea. And be wary of the auld lad living next door in Number 1. Albert Clarke's his name and he's a bit off, if you get my drift.' Mr. O'Toole was quite a find.

I managed to deliver forms to four of the ten houses on Liberty Terrace, which, as I was swiftly discovering, was a very good result. I dropped calling cards into the remaining six, ticked everything off in my Record Book.

The first house at the edge of Liberty Terrace was a comfortable-looking two-storey, pebble-dashed house with a rambling over-grown front garden. I opened and closed the front gate carefully. Leave nothing to chance, don't give anyone an excuse to complain about you, my Supervisor had warned. The young woman who answered the door turned out to be Laura O'Leary, the novelist whose writing classes I'd attended. She seemed glad to see me, and said she'd be happy to read more of my work whenever I was ready, so all in all, it was turning out to be a better day than I expected.

I was feeling fairly cheerful as I approached the next house — an early Victorian like ours, only much bigger — three storeys high, with two dormer windows instead of one. From the street, it looked like a giant's doll's house, perfectly painted in pale blue, with the right kind of sash windows, in glossy white. It had a garden too, bigger than our front yard, carefully tended, with wealthy-looking shrubs. The dormer windows were complete with what looked like the original finials and a perfect roof with exactly the right slates. I wouldn't have swapped our house for many others, especially after all the effort we'd made to keep it during bad times, but this house was a bigger, better version.

The wrought-iron gate opened easily and, again, I closed it carefully behind me. The right kind of tiled path, red and black squares led up to a shiny Royal blue door with stained glass panels.

The bell tinkled confidently when I pressed it and I waited a moment before I rang it again. I could see a figure advancing down the hallway through the glass, and then the door swung open.

A thin, olive-skinned woman with sleek dark hair in a sculpted bob stood there. About my own age, she wore huge dark glasses as if she'd recently been on a Mediterranean holiday and hadn't yet adjusted to being back. She wore an expensive white shirt — the kind that looks so simple you just know it's cost a lot — with black jeans and a pair of Ugg slippers. The whole effect was one of casual glamour.

'If you're collecting for charity you can bugger off,' she said, in a crass London accent.

'I'm not,' I said quickly, as she began to push the door closed. I held out my ID but she didn't even look at it. 'I'm your Census Enumerator, and I'll only take a few minutes of your time.'

She stared over my head, towards her front gate.

'I can't sign any forms today,' she said. 'You'll have to come back next week.'

Give them nothing to complain about, my Supervisor

had said. So there was nothing I could do except to recite the whole rigmarole, that I only needed to give her the form that day, tell her about the Census, what it was for, blah blah blah. My servility almost choked me.

Eventually she gave me her name and when she did, I thought for a moment that I'd misheard it. When I wrote it in my Record Book, I pressed so fiercely with my biro that, later on, I noticed that her name was embossed on the reverse of the page.

'Two females here,' she said, in answer to my question.

Maybe it wasn't her. Surely the dreaded Cynthia Stanton wouldn't be living with a female? From what I'd heard of Cynthia, all those years ago, she was only interested in men.

'Could I have a contact number?'

'I can't be doing with mobiles,' she said.

'A landline number, even? I'll need to collect the form after Census Day, so it would really help if I could call you beforehand to arrange a convenient time.'

'I'm always here,' she said.

'Fine. I'll just give you the form then.'

When I held out the form, she didn't take it. Instead, she took a few steps backwards into the house.

'Put it inside,' she said, as if I was a servant, waving vaguely at what turned out to be a hall table inside the door.

I still don't understand how I managed to calmly step forward and place the form gently where she'd indicated, because inside my head I felt like screaming. I stepped back and looked at her again.

'All you need to do is complete it on the actual night of the Census. Thank you very much for your time.' I shoved my Record Book in the dreadful bag and turned around to walk away. The front door slammed shut behind me as I fumbled with the gate.

It was her, I thought. I was convinced of it, though all I knew about Cynthia was the information I'd begged so tearfully out of Andrea, the restaurant manager, back in 2005. 'A supercilious English bitch,' Andrea had said. 'Don't worry. He'll get fed up of her soon enough. Or she'll get fed up of him.'

Here, she was, my nemesis, Cynthia, on my Census patch, with her perfectly preserved house and her good roof and those perfect dormer windows, with their perfectly formed finials and she was thin (maybe a bit too thin, but still), and glamorous and well-off and she had caused me so much heartbreak and had got away scot-free and she didn't have to worry about mending a roof and she didn't have to put up with errant crows or trudge the streets for extra cash like me.

'It's over,' James had said, when he finally admitted it. 'She's awful. She's like a vulture. I must have been out of my mind.' He stroked my stomach and told me it meant absolutely nothing and that I was the only one for him. My pregnancy was just beginning to show. We sold my place in Dublin, moved to Cork and never spoke of it again.

That night, I couldn't sleep. I came downstairs for a glass of milk and tried to read a novel. James came in the door at 2 a.m.

'You're still up?' he said. He went to the fridge and opened it.

'Not exactly,' I said. 'I was in bed but I couldn't sleep.'

'The crows again?' He poured himself a glass of wine and sat at the table opposite me.

'Too early for the crows. I'm overtired, that's all.'

'I work hard too, you know.' He slugged back some wine as if it were water and fumbled in his pocket for his vape.

'I'm not saying you don't.' He badly needed a haircut. He was too proud of his thick blond hair and too pleased when he noticed the receding hairlines of other men.

'We could have just patched the roof.' He sucked on his vape and the smoke obscured his face.

I was too weary to contradict him. 'I've organised it now, so...'

He pushed his fingers through his stupid hair and frowned. 'You're just a glutton for punishment,' he said.

After Census Day, there was no work for a week. Then I had to go back to every single house once more, to collect the completed forms. By the time I called to Cynthia's door, I still hadn't figured out what I might say or do to get revenge. She was wearing another pair of dark glasses, even though it was raining. The pretentious bitch; it was enough to make me grit my teeth.

'Call back later,' she said. 'I don't have time to find the form right now.'

I felt like a banshee ready to wail, but I forced myself to stay calm. I was so close, so close, to finishing this awful job and I knew I'd have to get the form from her before I made any kind of scene. I reminded myself that I was on the last lap and that I always finished what I started. Afterwards, once I'd got paid for this awful job, I'd have the money for my roof. Then I'd find a way to make her pay.

That afternoon, I called again. The door opened after a few minutes. A young girl of about Milo's age stood there, an unhappy, put-upon expression on her face. She was pale-skinned, with a scatter of freckles across her nose, and long butter-coloured hair pinned back on either side by a pink flower hair clip. She didn't look much like Cynthia.

'Yes?' she said as if I'd interrupted something important.

Well, I thought. She's got Cynthia's personality anyway.

'I called to collect the Census Form earlier,' I said. 'But the lady I met — your mother, is it? — couldn't find it.'

'Mum's always losing things,' the child said. She sounded as if she hated Cynthia, and that endeared her to me somewhat. 'It's so annoying.'

'It sure is,' I said. 'I like your hair clips, by the way.'

'Oh, thanks,' she said and stood up a little straighter. 'I got them in Claire's Accessories.'

'Should I give you another form?' I pulled a blank one from my wretched bag.

'Oh, is that what it looks like? Hang on. I know where it is.' Her smile crinkled up her face. There was something terribly familiar about that smile. 'I'll be back in two shakes.' She ran back into the dark depths of the hallway and in a few seconds she was back, waving the Census Form at me.

'Ta da!' she said triumphantly, like Milo did, the day he finally learnt to ride his bike.

I glanced through the form quickly, which was all an Enumerator was supposed to do. A quick check, to make sure all the sections were filled in and that the householder hadn't forgotten to sign at the back.

'Perfect,' I said. 'Thank you.' Part of me couldn't bear to look at her again and part of me wanted to keep on looking. The child looked so much like Milo that it scared me.

I traipsed off to the Hot Stuff Café and ordered a cappuccino. My hands trembled as I took Cynthia's Census Form out of the goddam bag. I read the whole thing once and then a second time, in case I was imagining things.

Person 1. Cynthia Stanton owned her house outright, which infuriated me. She wasn't married and she had one child. She was educated to Postgraduate level and was self-employed in PR and Marketing. She'd lived in Dublin a year ago and she'd lived there since 2003. Before that she'd lived in England. Her nationality was English, which I already knew.

Person 2. Cynthia's daughter was born in Dublin in 2006, three months after my son Milo's birth in Cork.

The builders came in July. The roof was done within a week. The new slates were perfect. The wooden surround of the dormer window looked exactly like the original, only better, and the finial was just as the original must have been.

But still I could not get a good night's sleep. I woke too early every morning. I missed the sound of the crows as I lay alone in bed, in a desperate kind of silence.

PENTHOUSE

Lorcan Hickey walked unsteadily down the steps of the plane, into a torrent of rain. I should have remembered it always fucking rains in Cork, he thought, as he lurched towards the terminal, squinting through his rain-drenched Raybans.

Through the door marked 'WELCOME TO CORK', Lorcan gasped and blinked, shaking the rain off his leather jacket. His jeans felt damp and tight and he wondered if they could possibly have shrunk. He took his Raybans off and wiped them on his t-shirt but when he put them on again everything still seemed blurred. Never mind; he had a pair of lighter shades in his suitcase.

Advance upstairs. Passport Control. No queue, thank fuck. The passengers ahead of him were already bustling through. The security guy gave him a friendly smile, took a cursory look at his passport and waved him on. A change from the good old days and the suspicious glares, thought Lorcan. This guy seemed more like a representative of Bord Fáilte than an immigration officer.

It was many years since Lorcan had flown into Cork and during that time a brand-new airport terminal had been built to replace the old one. Lorcan felt oddly disappointed that the imitation fireplace was no longer there to greet him in the baggage retrieval area; that hokey old fireplace with its low unreal flames, below a 'Céad Míle Fáilte' sign in decorative old-fashioned script. He remembered a time when he and the lads had come back from London like conquering heroes for an Irish tour, after their first big break and signing with a major label. Wrecked from all the drink, plus cocaine snorted hastily before the flight, they had hung around at the fireplace while the tour manager waited for their multiple pieces of luggage — bags of leads and microphones, drums in flight cases, guitars. At first the fireplace became the focus of their piss-taking; then, to the horror of most of the unwilling audience, they'd begun to wail a made-up version of 'Come all ye maidens young and fair' that was pure filth. Come and come again and take it in the mouth. Let me at that maidenhead. What a fucking laugh. They almost got arrested.

As Lorcan moved away from where he thought the fireplace should be, a hefty woman in a flowered plastic raincoat turned to look at him. Dyed brown hair with a line of dirty grey showing at the parting, murky makeup on a bloated face, recognition dawning.

Oh Jesus, he thought, dementedly. Do I know that woman? Vague inkling. A fat girl with bad skin and plaits, huge tits. Musk oil and availability oozing from her. Majella Lane, the Entertainments Officer in UCC back in the day. She'd put his first band on in the college bar, what, thirty years ago or more? He'd shagged her a few times to land that first ever gig, and left at the end of the night with someone else.

Desperate for an escape, he looked around and saw the toilet doors marked 'Mná' and 'Fir' and 'Disabled.' He dodged off; badly needed a piss anyway, after all that vodka on the plane. Ah, urine streaming out feeling better now wash hands maybe brush my teeth ah feck, the washbag's in the fucking suitcase no worries the good thing about vodka is you can't really smell it anyway. He remembered he'd turned his phone to 'silent' on the plane, so he took it out and checked it. One text. It was from Jake.

> I'm going to be late. Traffic bad. I'll be
> there as soon as possible. Sincere apologies.

So formal. Still, it was only to be expected. When his son got to know him better, he'd chill out.

Peering out of the gents, he saw the baggage carousel judder into action and crank up. A bulging orange rucksack jiggered helplessly at the brink of the void before dropping onto the moving rubber belt. More suitcases and holdalls — mainly black and grey—toppled after it and shivered along.

Majella lunged forward and heaved a strangulated brown suitcase off the circling belt. She looked around as if in search of Lorcan, so he ducked back into the Gents. This is silly, he thought. He washed his hands again, before walking out in what he hoped was a nonchalant, casual way, just in time to see Majella's rear view as she trundled her brown suitcase off towards the green 'Nothing to Declare' zone. All clear. Safe to approach.

Not many people were waiting for their luggage now. A young woman in jeans, wearing a baby in a purple sling, stood next to him. She stared, hawk-eyed, at the moving carousel.

'You'd think they'd get their asses in gear,' she said. 'I thought they'd be out straight away with my pushchair.'

Finally, only one small black bag remained, going round and round until a young man appeared to retrieve it. No sign of Lorcan's suitcase. Ah feck.

The tannoy announced the arrival of a flight from Manchester. More passengers traipsed into the baggage hall and a neighbouring carousel began to turn.

Only Lorcan and the young woman with the baby still waited anxiously at the first—by now completely barren—baggage carousel. From its purple pouch, the baby stared lugubriously at Lorcan, who had an urge to stick his tongue out, but it looked like a baby that might cry and Lorcan, who had an aversion to babies in general, could tolerate crying babies even less.

'If they've lost the baby's buggy I'll go mental,' said the young woman.

Just then, Lorcan's suitcase thurrumped onto the carousel; a battered limegreen Samsonite plastered with raddled travel stickers from long-forgotten tours. Suddenly, joyously, Lorcan guessed his luggage had been searched for drugs. The powers-that-be had recognised him: the punk who knocked the plaster head off a Virgin Mary statue on *The Late Late Show* in 1985; the notorious rocker who had had a major hit single back in the day (well, number 4 in Ireland and number 29 in the UK). Home sweet home.

Outside the airport, the rain had stopped and a weak sun shone through the clouds like a scene of resurrection in Lorcan's old primary school catechism. The air smelt of wet grass and petrol and cigarettes; the tobacco smell emanating from a couple of young lads who loitered, smoking roll-ups, beneath the red and white no smoking sign on the wall.

Jake had said he'd be driving a black Audi, and every

time a black car drove through the yellow barrier Lorcan felt nervous, since he had no idea what an Audi looked like. He didn't drive. No need in London, he told people, but truth to tell, he'd been too wasted to learn to drive when he had had the money for a car. He'd always been scared of driving anyway since his old man had tried to teach him long ago — back in Ballincollig when he was seventeen — and made him feel like a useless piece of shit.

The young lads looked to be in their late teens and seemed to be in the midst of a quietly intense argument, occasionally glancing over at Lorcan in a way that unnerved him. The red-haired lad wore a denim jacket and the other, thin-faced and pale, wore a zipped-up grey hoodie. They both wore shellsuit pants that looked as if they were made of plastic. A right pair of gurriers, thought Lorcan. Gurriers. Knackers. Norries. Langers. Toerags. They were probably discussing how to mug him. He should not have worn his leather jacket.

The lads moved a few cautious paces closer and Lorcan was about to run, when the red-haired lad looked directly at him. 'Em, just want to say there, we love your music like. I mean, *Elevator Lust*, that was a magic album, man.'

'Fucking brilliant, it was,' said the other, looking at the ground. 'Mighty.'

'Thanks lads,' said Lorcan. He felt almost guilty now, for thinking the lads were low-lifes. He'd been called a gurrier more than once himself when he was their age.

'Sorry to bother you, like, only we're huge fans... I'm Nazz, by the way.' The red-haired lad stretched out his hand awkwardly and Lorcan shook it. 'He's Bunny.'

Bunny smiled shyly from underneath his hood, and for a brief moment, his upper row of teeth protruded, rabbit-like.

'Thing is, we're the Jupiter Scumbags and we're doing a gig in Cork tonight,' said Nazz. 'Any chance you'd come? We can put you on the guest list, buy you a pint, whatever.'

'Yeah,' said Bunny.

'Maybe you could do a bit of jamming with us? It'd be fucken amazeballs,' said Nazz. 'You got a flyer, Bunny?'

Bunny took a crumpled flyer out of his pocket, straightened it out and handed it to Lorcan.

'We're on at ten. Going to be a great night,' said Nazz.

Lorcan held the wrinkled piece of paper a short distance from his face but he could read no more than the words in large type — 'Cypress Avenue' — and he didn't want to hold it out and peer at it from arm's length, like an old fucker. 'Ah sorry lads. I'm only here for a family thing.'

'Pity,' said Nazz. 'We just thought we'd chance asking you, seeing as you're here. What you up to these days, Lorcan?'

'As a matter of fact, I'm working on a rock opera,' said Lorcan. 'It's about the rise and fall and rise again of a charismatic...'

'Where the fuck were you?' demanded a female voice from a distance. A magnificent, curvaceous young woman in biker jacket and jeans stood several yards away. Her raven-black hair was streaked with metallic blue, shaved above her ears and long at the back. From that distance, Lorcan could make out the words emblazoned on her t-shirt:

JESUS LOVES YOU
EVERYONE ELSE THINKS YOU'RE AN ARSEHOLE

'Great t-shirt,' Lorcan said as she approached.

'Lena, can you believe it? Lorcan Hickey.'

'The Merkins, right?' she said, almost callously.

'Yeah,' said Lorcan.

'My sister Lena,' Nazz explained. 'Just flown in from Manchester. She's our backing vocalist.' He turned to Lena. 'We invited him to the gig but he can't make it.'

'Pity,' she said.

'Well, we'd better head off,' said Nazz. 'Fucking great to meet you, Lorcan.'

As they turned to leave, Lorcan found he didn't want them to go. 'Hang on lads, have ye got a demo?' he asked.

'We've stuff up on YouTube — we could send you the links.'

'What's the name of your band again?'

'The Jupiter Scumbags.'

'Wait a minute. I'm going to ring my manager.' Lorcan nodded importantly, tapped his phone a few times and held it to his ear.

'Hey Quentin, the eagle has landed,' he said.

'Lorcan. What do you want? If it's about that rock opera thing...'

'No, no, that's all in hand. Listen. I've just come across a young Cork band called the Jupiter Scumbags.'

'And?'

'You got to check them out. They'll send you their demo.'

'I told you before, Lorcan. Quit wasting my time.'

'So you can expect to hear from them. Email or whatever.' Lorcan nodded confidently at the lads.

'Whatever.'

'You'll check it out when it arrives?'

'No.'

'Excellent,' said Lorcan and ended the call. He recited Quentin's email address while Nazz typed it into his phone. Nazz and Bunny were practically quivering with excitement. Only Lena seemed calm.

A black car pulled into a designated parking space. The driver, a clean-shaven, anxious man in his early thirties, got out. Carefully dressed in jeans and a well-cut jacket, he wore a shirt with no tie.

'Hi Lorcan. Sorry I'm late.'

Lorcan had no idea how to greet his son. 'Long time no see,' he ventured.

'Sure is. Last time we met, I was only two,' said Jake. 'Sit in. I'll put your suitcase in the boot.'

As Lorcan ensconced himself in the passenger seat, he barely noticed the girl passing by, dragging a suitcase awkwardly behind her, her baby whinging now from the folds of its purple sling.

As Jake drove out of the airport and onto a road that led to the city centre, Lorcan had a chance to study him. Jake seemed utterly recognisable; something about his face; those hands on the steering wheel; like Lorcan's hands; a wedding band; he must be married.

'I've organised an apartment for you for the week,' said Jake.

'I'm not staying with you?'

'It's easier this way,' Jake paused. 'I think you'll like it,' he added. 'So long as you don't have a problem with heights. You don't, do you?'

'I don't think so.'

Jake bit the side of his lip as he drove. Just like Siofra, who used to bite the skin inside her mouth whenever she was troubled or puzzled. Lorcan used to tell her that if she wasn't careful she'd end up with two big holes in her cheeks. He imagined Siofra lying in her coffin, eyelids fluttering open, her eyes staring out at him accusingly from her beautiful face. For she had been beautiful, though he had not fully realised that at the time.

Jake drove skilfully, at an even pace. As they reached the city, he spoke again.

'You'll see it in a couple of seconds.'

'What did you call it again?' said Lorcan.

'The Elysian. It's the highest building in Ireland now.'

A tall conglomeration of towers studded with glass squares loomed ahead. The Elysian would not look out of place in Milan or Lisbon, thought Lorcan. It was almost unimaginable that anyone would have conceived of such a building in Cork. Jake turned right and then, carefully, right again. He used a card to raise a barrier and drove into an underground car park, where he eased the car into parking space 17.

'There's a communal garden in the centre,' Jake said. 'Very nice. Very Zen. But first I'll show you where you're staying.'

In the elevator, Jake pressed the top button. 'It's quiet here. Most of the apartments are empty — people can't afford them.'

The main living area of the penthouse suite was a double-height space. One wall, almost entirely made of glass, opened onto a balcony. It was full of light now, as the cold May sun had come from behind the clouds to shine over a panoramic view of Cork City to the east. The River Lee stretched out below, and a tall ship was moored by the quay. Everything seemed familiar but distant.

The vast sitting-room was furnished with a basket chair dangling from the ceiling like the one from a '70s advert for nylon tights, an L-shaped couch in tan leather, a metal and glass coffee table, a cut-glass vase filled with artificial orchids on a large dining table, a Rothko print on the wall, a gigantic flat-screen TV.

'Amazing.' It was the kind of city pad Lorcan imagined a Russian oligarch might own.

'I figured you were used to staying in fancy places.'

'Yeah,' said Lorcan. It was nothing like his housing association flat in Holloway.

'So, it's okay?'

'Brilliant,' Lorcan managed. 'Is this your own place?'

'God no. A friend lent it to me.'

'Oh.'

'The place is empty, so he let me have it for the week.'

Jake certainly knew the right people, thought Lorcan, jubilantly. He'd only have to pitch the thing properly and Jake would immediately understand that to invest in his father's rock opera was a win-win situation.

'You're doing so well.'

'I'm doing okay.'

'I googled you. Amazing. My son, the youngest ever managing director of PharmaShaman Pharmaceuticals.'

'Yeah, I've been fortunate to get that job. I was anxious to move back to Cork as well. Had enough of Dublin.'

'Selling legal drugs, ha ha.' This was the wrong note, Lorcan realised. He tried again. 'Your company — does it take an interest in the Arts, at all?'

'We sponsor a few local things. Midsummer Festival, Christmas in Bishop Lucey Park, that kind of thing. The kitchen is through here.'

Jake led Lorcan into the kitchen, where he patted the black marble counter.

'Designed by Porsche, would you believe.'

'Nice,' said Lorcan.

'I got in some milk, butter, oranges — there's a juicer in a cupboard — bread and cheese from the English Market. Would you like a drink? I mean tea or coffee or something? I didn't get wine or anything. I presumed...'

'Oh no, no, I never touch the stuff now. Clean as a whistle,

I am. Clean as a new pin.' Shut up, Lorcan said in his head. 'Squeaky clean.'

'I was surprised when you contacted me. Not saying you're not welcome, but when you didn't come for the funeral?'

'Ah no. Sorry. I just thought it wasn't...'

'Mam wouldn't have minded. She always gave everyone a second chance. I miss her terribly.'

Jake's phone rang. He bit the inside of his mouth again as he pressed a button to accept the call. 'Yeah, I'm with him now. What is it?' He listened for a moment. His face changed from anxious to stricken. 'Shit. I'll be there in a few minutes.' He put the phone back in his pocket and picked up his car keys from the kitchen counter. 'I'm sorry. I've got to go. It's an emergency.' He headed for the door, then whirled round. 'I nearly forgot. The entrance code and the wifi password are on the notepad next to the sink. I wrote the mobile number of the building superintendent down too; any problems, he's on the ground floor and he knows you're here for the week. Sorry about this. I'll text you once I know what's happening.'

Alone in the Elysian penthouse, all Lorcan could hear was a low sinister hum; from the heating maybe, or from the super-sleek stainless steel fridge. It was too quiet. He contemplated turning on the TV but the remote controls unnerved him. He opened the balcony doors and stood outside. The wind had risen and the sun had retreated behind those biblical clouds. It was going to rain again. It was cold. Far too cold for May.

Siofra. She had been — yes — his first love. He couldn't remember any other woman with such clarity. Jake called his manager about the funeral two years ago. Lorcan had been skint, and, anyway, he couldn't face it. Only now, he fully understood that she was dead and that he had failed her yet again. Why the hell did Jake feck off and leave him stranded here? What the fuck was he going to do for the night?

He'd do some work. That's what he'd do. Then he'd go out, spend a few of those euros, get a bite to eat, have an early night. He settled in, opened his battered suitcase, took out his heavy old laptop bag and set it on the kitchen counter. Then, from the bag, he drew out the handwritten score for the rock opera he'd almost completed — well, the first draft of it anyway.

This must work. It has to be a success. *There's nothing else I know how to do.* He sat there in the spotless kitchen and tried to concentrate on the problem with the chorus at the end of Act One, but the musical notation began to blur and he had absolutely no idea how to continue. The only rock opera he had ever gone to see had been a travesty; overblown, pretentious and deeply uncool. As he thought about this, the notes he'd carefully written by hand began to crotchet and quaver all over the pages, and the lyrics underneath seemed ludicrously vague.

He closed his eyes for a moment, but all he could see was Siofra's shocked face. It was 1981. They were living in a flat in Kentish Town. Siofra's work had sent her to Paris, but she came home a day early and found him wrapped around a Polish groupie in the kingsize pine bed she'd bought three weeks before. The Merkins from Outer Space had been big in Poland. Siofra was two months pregnant. He hadn't known.

Siofra's beautiful face. Her tears. Her blue-grey eyes assessing him and finding him entirely wanting. He could do with a drink or something stronger. He remembered his own parents, long dead, and the cold house in Ballincollig he'd escaped from. His father Maurice Hickey, ex-army officer, staunch Charlie Haughey supporter, chairman of the Pigs and Bacon Commission, whose disapproval of Lorcan turned into violent dislike after he dropped out of college. His mother, unable to cope, weak and deluded on Valium, always called him 'her pet' but where was she when the strap lashed down on the buttocks? Smoking her Silk Cuts furtively in the straggled yard, that's where.

God, he needed a drink. In a frenzy he opened and closed cupboard doors, the fridge, the freezer, even the built-in wardrobes in the bedrooms. No alcohol anywhere.

Fuck it, I may as well head out and get a drink. Least I deserve. Fresh t-shirt; quick check in the mirror; lift the chin; draw in the stomach; great bone structure, the military crewcut suited him; fine and dandy; out he went.

After a reasonable curry and several bottles of Singha in the Indian Palace, Lorcan felt more like himself. A short walk would do him the world of good, he reckoned, before he returned to the eerie quiet of the Elysian. As he passed by a small side street, someone called his name.

'Wow, Lorcan Hickey, you legend. You made it!'

There was Nazz, waving at him. Bunny was there too. So was Lena of the blue-black hair, resplendent in a black leather minidress and high boots.

'We just finished the sound-check. Come in and have a drink.'

Pint short pint short pint short shynt port shynt port.

Yeah, lads, it's Lorcan, lead singer of the Merkins from Outer Space. You're a fuckin' legend Lorcan. I'd never have got into music only for you. Got all your albums. On vinyl. The originals. Me older brother was well into the Merkins. The Blue Goldfish *album. Fuckin amazeballs. That* Late Late Show's *on YouTube, you know, the one with you doing wreck to the holy statue; Gay*

Byrne's face! Sure of course you'll do a guest spot?

. OF COURSE... It was show time on a small stage in a room above a pub in Cork and the Jupiter Scumbags belted unevenly into the first song and the second and then they got a bit tighter and the room was reeling a bit, the small crowd swaying — twenty, max — Lorcan drank a bit more, Nazz called his name AND OUR SPECIAL GUEST THE LEGENDARY LORCAN HICKEY and everyone cheered and Lorcan jumped off his bar stool and raced onto the stage and he could barely hear himself above the sound of the drums and bass and guitar but was more or less in tune as he hollered out the mixed-up lyrics of his major hit 'The Screws Are Loose' and the machine worked and the Jupiter Scumbags were making a fair old hand of it and Lena was doing a bit of backing vocals and they were gunning it now and the barely-there crowd was up on the old hind legs dancing, one more verse, almost there, nearly the end, he waved his arm up and down and the band stopped playing as one, all tight, just right, one big full stop and the microphone stand fell to the floor... an explosion of applause... Lorcan, still grasping the microphone, roared into it, 'Thanks, you fucking lunatics!' and his voice boomed and the crowd called 'More, more,' but the Jupiter Scumbags didn't know how to play any other Merkins' numbers so Nazz said 'Same again' and this time they drove right into 'The Screws Are Loose' and it was even better — a song about frustration, about things that didn't work properly, including Lorcan's head, a line in it about nails falling out of a cross so even the Crucifixion was a balls-up — and, at the end of the song, Lorcan fell face forward flat on the stage, arms outstretched like a crucified Christ who's fallen off his cross (just like he'd done that one time he played at Glastonbury, but never seriously thought he'd have the nerve to do again) and the place went apeshit crazy and Lorcan got up and bowed like a small child at the Feis and walked off the stage. He felt dirty, filthy, sweaty, hung-over, spent... and all he wanted was to do it all over again.

There was a kind of tidal wave to the events that followed, but somehow Lorcan was ferried in glory back to the Elysian by the Jupiter Scumbags and a handful of supporters, having munificently purchased drink from the Cypress Avenue bar with most of his dwindling supply of euros. A ferrety-faced dealer from Dublin came with them. There was a deal of excitement in the Penthouse that night; bottles and cans popped open, joints rolled, excited discovery of bread and cheese in the kitchen.

'I gotta bit a coke alright,' the ferret-face said, producing a wrap. 'And I got deese little lads.' He took two jam jars out of his jacket pocket. Each jar was full of magic mushrooms floating in a clear liquid. On each jar was a white handwritten label. One label read, '2016— *bouncy*' in blue biro. The other, in the same handwriting, bore the mystifying words, '2017— *quiet*.'

'Deese here are your introvairted kind a shrooms, and deese ones from tootowsananturteen, dey're a more lively, rockin' trip,' said the Dubliner.

A lively rockin' trip, decided Lorcan and slurped some down, parting with the last of his euros. For a short while, nothing much happened except the making of toast and disorganised slicing of cheese and investigation of Lorcan's ageing laptop because it was the only source of music they had and Lorcan began to dance and come up and it was a lively rockin' trip until he had to stop and cry and then be swarmed with pure love by the Jupiter Scumbags and dance again— umpteen times to 'We Are Family'—while the walls of the Penthouse turned from smooth and pale, switching back and forth from bright yellow to the mottled texture of old banana skins, and the fridge jiggered along with the music.

In the master bedroom lay Lena of the blue-black hair. It was 5 a.m. Surely an invitation, Lorcan thought, as he lay down alongside her and kissed the nape of her neck. As he began to lick her ear, she moaned sleepily and turned on her back to look at him.

'Jesus,' she said and sat up, blinking, one of her jet-black eyelashes askew.

'Relax,' he said and patted the quilt.

'Fuck off, Grandad,' she said. She picked up her high boots and left.

When Jake arrived at 2 p.m. the following afternoon, the last of Lorcan's new acquaintances had slunk out and slid away (apart from Bunny, still retching in the loo).

'Jesus Christ,' said Jake. 'The place is wrecked.'

'It's not too bad. I'll have it sorted in no time.' Lorcan's hands had an old man's tremor as he made a pot of coffee and spilt some on the black marble counter.

'Now, I need to talk to you about this rock opera I'm putting on. See, I'm looking for a backer...'

He looked around for his musical score, for the rock opera that would change his fortune. It lay on the kitchen counter as if it had been tortured. Brown splashes of beer, a scorch mark, probably from a fallen joint, part of a footprint. He picked it up and waved it at Jake.

'A backer?' Jake stared at Lorcan. 'Is that... That's what you came to talk about?'

'Well, partly. What's the problem? You seem a bit upset.'

'Upset? Of course I'm upset.'

'Look, I came all this way to see you...'

'London isn't "all this way"', Jake said, and the expression in his blue-grey eyes was exactly like Siofra's, the last time she'd looked upon Lorcan.

1984, it was. He'd come 'to sort things out'. Siofra was in her parents' sitting room, sitting on the couch with two-year old Jake on her lap. She bit the inside of her lip, as she listened to him. One-off payment. Confidentiality agreement. Harsh realities. The music business. His image. No hard feelings. Really, the fault lay with Lorcan's manager Quentin and the lawyer. They hadn't told him how to explain it properly. Lorcan remembers Siofra's mother taking the crying child out of the room, Siofra's brother-in-law Jim, entering, like a bouncer, and that look on Siofra's beautiful face before she stood up and walked out.

'I'm sorry about the mess,' he said to Jake now.

'Sorry isn't enough.'

Lorcan felt suddenly angry. 'Don't you know who I am? What did you expect when you just fucked off and left me to fend for myself?'

'Expect?' Jake stood there, chewing frantically at the inside of his mouth. 'What did I expect? I thought you came to make amends.' He walked towards the door, as if to leave. Then he stopped and turned to stare at Lorcan.

'Lorcan, listen to me.' He spoke in a cold, clear voice. 'It was my wife on the phone yesterday. Our son had suspected meningitis. Myself and Donna had to take him to hospital.'

'Your son? You have a son?'

'Yes. Your grandson.'

'I have a grandson?'

'He's six months old. He's beautiful.' Jake brushed what might have been a tear from his eye. 'So there I was in the early hours of the morning, stuck in the hospital, waiting and hoping that my child would be all right. He is, not that you've bothered to ask. I had my laptop with me so I googled you — just for something to do. And what did I find, but a brand new YouTube clip. Some unbelievably efficient member of the Cork music scene put it up at 2 a.m. You better have a look.'

He turned to Lorcan's laptop and typed something in, then swivelled it so that Lorcan had a clear view of the screen.

There is the diminutive crowd in Cypress Avenue moshing in front of the tiny stage where now the camera zones in on Lorcan, his gut protruding between his too tight jeans and his t-shirt, his scalp shining baldly through his marine cut — oh the horror begins — he's leaping around like a lunatic, gesticulating as he roars 'The Screws Are Loose' completely out of tune while Lena, behind him, points her index finger to her temple and turns it round and round, then points at Lorcan and raises her eyebrows as she sings, mocking him to the audience. Nazz, oblivious, wreaks havoc on guitar, the drummer flakes and flails and Bunny frets intensively on bass while Lena rolls her eyes behind Lorcan and makes a wanking motion with one hand... the camera zones in on the handful of people in the audience, and Lorcan had no idea until now that they are all laughing *at* him, not *with* him, that he is nothing but a joke, and when he throws himself upon the floor some of them are so creased with laughter they look as if they will throw up. From laughing. At him.

'You were all piss and vinegar last night, weren't you?' said Jake, caustically. 'I gave you a second chance like Mam did. But you know what? That's it. I'm too busy for this shit. I'm busy raising my kid and trying to make sure I don't end up being an arsehole like you. So please leave. You've one hour to get out of here.'

'Ah Jake...'

'Give me the keys. I'll lock up.'

'What? But...'

'No more buts,' Jake said. The door closed firmly behind him.

In the kitchen, Lorcan stood for a moment, bewildered. He forced his attention back to the frozen image on his laptop and fumbled at the keyboard to quit the awful image and slam the damn thing shut. He went upstairs to find the battered lime-green Samsonite and threw the rank-smelling clothing from the night before inside. In the bathroom, Bunny was still there, his head hanging over the toilet bowl. 'Bugger off,' Lorcan said. The pallid creature groaned, pushed himself into a standing position and limped out. Lorcan shoved his toothbrush and toothpaste into his washbag and pushed it into the suitcase.

In the kitchen he found the elderly laptop and placed it in the suitcase. He found his leather jacket and put it on. He checked the pockets warily. At least he hadn't been robbed. His wallet, passport and plane ticket were still in the inside pocket.

The musical score still lay on the kitchen counter amid empty cans, stubbed out cigarettes, crusts of toast, crumbs of cheese. He picked the manuscript up and flicked through its beer-stained pages. The lyrics were indecipherable, the lopsided musical notes crocheted and quavered before his bloodshot eyes.

He folded and refolded the bedraggled manuscript, tried to shove it into his jacket pocket, but it wouldn't fit. 'Ah feck it,' he said. 'Blast it, dammit, to hell with it.' He hurled the misshapen score in the direction of the kitchen bin, picked up his suitcase and stomped out of the apartment. The door slammed shut behind him.

EZINNA'S FLAMBOYANT TREE

Early on a Saturday morning, Ezinna pushed her baby, little Blessing, in a buggy, along a small but busy street in Cork. Her son, Joel, straggled sulkily behind them. He was twelve and no longer wanted to be seen in town with her but was too young to be left at home.

The Farmer's Market on the Coal Quay was already in full swing. Stalls lined the wide pavement, where traders sold hot food and drinks, cheese and fish, vegetables and fruit, bread and cakes, candles, soap and flowers. The early risers—those denizens of the city who hadn't been in the pubs until all hours the night before, and mothers, like Ezinna, whose children never allowed them to sleep late—were wandering around the stalls with an easy familiarity, stopping now and then to chat or to ponder on what to buy. The market reminded Ezinna of home, though the goods on sale were different here.

As Ezinna ambled past a stall displaying an array of flowering plants, she stopped to look. The colours of the flowers—yellows, pinks, oranges and purples—cheered her. Ezinna loved bright colours and singing; two of the many things Joel disliked about his mother.

A small tree-like plant with bright red flowers sat in a large pot in the centre of the display. The colour of the flame-red petals reminded her of the blossoms on the big Flamboyant tree that stood next to her childhood home in Kaduna. As a child, she always thought of that huge tree as her very own. Sturdy and tall, it grew right next to the house, stretching up into the bright blue sky until it was higher than the roof, exploding with bright red-orange flowers every springtime.

Of course, this little tree was not the same. It was small, for one thing, and the petals were not at all the same shape —yet the colour reminded her so much of the Flamboyant tree back home that she suddenly felt a pain in her heart. She used to sit underneath the outstretched branches in the long warm evenings when she was young and still a dreamer, before she met Obi and got married, before all the trouble began, before they left everything behind and fled.

She pushed the buggy close to the stall and put her foot down on the brake. Blessing, thankfully, was asleep. She leaned forward to see the label on the plant pot. *Japanese Quince, Chaenomeles Japonica Nicoline, €15.*

Joel tugged at her sleeve. 'Come on, let's go home now.' He spoke as if he had always lived in Cork. She knew he no longer liked to be seen with her in town, that he was ashamed of her accent which sounded wrong, that he had become embarrassed by the bright clothing that she liked to wear, that he wished she would fade into the background and disappear. He longed to be the same as all the other boys in his class—she knew that too—but it was, of course, impossible. Sometimes this depressed her and made her feel even lonelier than usual.

Sometimes it made her cross. At least Blessing was still too young to despise her.

She shrugged Joel's arm away and looked again. €15 was far too expensive, she thought. If she bought the plant today, she would have to dig into her secret savings to pay for food next week. Her savings were tucked inside the pages of her Bible, money that she kept for unexpected expenses and emergencies like the time that Joel was invited to a birthday party and had to bring a present. She looked at the little tree again, and longed for it.

'I like that little tree,' she said out loud.

'It's not a tree. It's a shrub,' said Joel.

How would she bring this tree home? She would balance it, she thought, at the back of the buggy; the pot would fit in the netted pouch at the back, where she sometimes placed her shopping. The tree was about three feet tall. The branches might get a little damaged, the flowers might get bruised, but, no, she would be careful. It was only a short walk home. People might stare at her and think it odd, but she was used to that.

'Lovely colour, isn't it?' the lady said from behind her stall. She had a nice round face and looked familiar. 'I'll give it to you for €10.'

'Thank you,' said Ezinna. 'I'll take it.'

Ezinna knew that she should count her blessings. She and Obi had arrived in Ireland in 2015 and had been granted refugee status three years later. It took another four months for all the paperwork to come through, so they could begin their brand new life as citizens. They had lived, for most of that time, in the Direct Provision Centre on the Kinsale Road. It had been difficult for all of them, especially for Joel, who sometimes looked at them as if he wished he wasn't theirs. Blessing had been a surprise and something of a shock. Ezinna still found it difficult to understand how she and Obi could have made her, for intimacy between herself and Obi had not often been possible – in that one room in the hostel, mostly she remembers lying anxiously awake, while Joel slept and Obi snored.

When the time came for them to leave the Direct Provision Centre, it had proved difficult to find a place to rent. They would have to live in the city for Obi had found work there and they did not own a car. Marie, one of a group of Irish volunteers who visited the Direct Provision Centre, had driven Ezinna to her hospital appointments when she was expecting Blessing and had given Obi a character refence for his job. It was Marie who brought Ezinna and Obi to see the house on Liberty Terrace, for she knew the landlord, and had spoken to him on their behalf.

Liberty Terrace was a row of small red brick houses, all joined together, with front doors that opened right onto the street. Most of the other houses in the row were neatly painted, but Number 3 had evidently been neglected.

'It's probably as good as you're likely to get, within your budget,' Marie said, as they waited outside for the landlord to arrive. Ezinna knew by now that Marie always told the truth.

The landlord was a thin, grey man who looked as if no one ever fed him. He struggled to unlock the door. 'A bit of washing up liquid on the key will sort that out,' he said. 'Sitting room, dining room and kitchen downstairs. Three bedrooms and a bathroom up above.'

'Lovely area,' Marie said. 'But the place could do with a lick of paint.'

'I don't mind ye painting it,' the landlord said. 'So long as the colours aren't too bright.'

The small kitchen at the back of the house opened onto a dilapidated backyard. A thin and fractured layer of concrete covered most of the ground, with brave weeds emerging here and there between the cracks. For easy maintenance, the landlord said, but it looked bleak and grey.

'I can get you a few pot plants, make it pretty,' whispered Marie.

At least there was a green space right across the street, a small park, with a few mature trees dotted here and there, where Ezinna could bring the children to play. Two larger houses stood alone in mature gardens nearby. If God was good, perhaps there would be children in this neighbourhood. Good children, of Joel's age, who would allow him to be a friend.

Ezinna's husband Obi worked as a waiter in a busy restaurant in the centre of the city. He had been glad to get the job, even though he had been a police sergeant back home. Now he worked long hours and tried hard to make a good impression, but despite his efforts to get on well with his fellow-workers, he suspected he did not get his fair share of the tips. Ezinna begged him to say nothing — to let it go, for now.

When Obi came home late from work on Saturday night and saw the little tree she'd bought, sitting on the kitchen floor, he shook his head.

'Why you spend my money foolishly, woman? There's no place to plant it here.'

Ezinna felt ashamed. She picked up her tree in its plastic pot and set it down outside in the bleak backyard. It was dark outside, apart from a square of yellow light slanting from the kitchen window. 'Obi is right. It was silly to buy you,' she told the tree, as it sat there, next to the dustbin. 'Really, you are nothing like the beautiful trees we have back home.' Then she was sorry for her harsh words, for the tree looked desolate in the shadows, with only the ageing rotary clothes line and the dustbin to keep it company. 'I am lonely too,' she admitted to the tree, and tears welled up in her eyes. The little tree nodded its leaves at her as if it understood.

Ezinna had made some friends in Direct Provision but they were scattered now. Some, like Deborah and Florence, had moved or been moved to other places around the country. Others, worse still, had been sent home. 'We are the lucky ones,' she told the tree. 'We are citizens now, and safe.' She wiped her eyes and set her face so that Obi would not notice she'd been crying, but by the time she went inside, he had already gone to bed.

That night, Ezinna dreamed about home. In the morning, when she began to tell Obi about her dream, he refused to talk about it. 'We are here and we can never go back,' he said. 'There is no point in remembering.'

The little tree grew and grew. To Ezinna's disappointment it grew outward more than upward. Soon the little tree — or shrub, as Joel said, self-righteously — was falling sideways out of the pot and beginning to look needy. This little tree did not wish to stand in a tiny pot in a raddled concrete yard. Ezinna feared that unless her little tree was given enough space, it would surely die.

After everyone in the house was asleep, Ezinna got out of bed, put her sandals on and went downstairs. She took a soup ladle from her kitchen, since she did not possess a shovel or a spade. She took her door key from the wooden bowl on the kitchen table and put it in her pocket. She walked outside into the dim light of the street and across the road to the small green park. She went over to the place she'd chosen, near the biggest tree. Slowly she began to ladle clumps of grass out of the ground, and then dig further into the damp soil, working quietly until the hole was big enough for her tree. Then she put her ladle down and went back to her house.

'My little tree, my little tree, come with me,' she sang, underneath her breath, as she carried her shrub, with its delicate red flowers, out to the park. 'My little tree, I have made a new home for thee.' Ever so gently, she prised her tree and the damp soil that surrounded it from its container, and placed it gently in the hole that she had made. She pushed handfuls of earth around the base of the plant, and tamped the soil down. She replaced the clumps of grass so that it seemed her little tree had always grown there. She went back into her house with the empty plastic plant pot, and filled a jug of water from the tap. Outside again, she poured the water around the base of the tree.

'My tree, my tree, my tree,' she sang. 'Here is a little drink for thee.' She sauntered home with the jug in her hand, still singing. She had not sung a silly song for ages.

Some days later, the sun was shining, so Ezinna took Blessing and Joel out to the green park after lunch. While Blessing dozed in her pushchair, Joel kicked his football around aimlessly, hoping, Ezinna supposed, that someone would eventually turn up to play with him. She took out a large plastic bottle filled with tap water and began to pour it around the base of her tree. It had spread outwards and upwards and was still in bloom. On the whole, it still looked very pleasing. 'My tree, my tree, my tree,' she sang as she poured the last of the water around the roots.

The old man who lived in Number 2 walked towards them. As usual, he wore a suit, as if he was on his way to church. Unlike the other neighbours, Mr O'Toole had called to the door to welcome them when they moved into their house. However, he had asked too many questions and Ezinna and Obi had felt intimidated, at first. They feared he was the kind of man they knew from back home; the kind of man who always wanted to know everything about everyone; the kind of man who could cause trouble if he wanted to. But Joel had consulted the old man on a history project and since then they'd become good friends.

'Hey Deckie,' said Joel.

Deckie stopped and stood there, smiling.

'How's the form?' he said to Joel.

'Grand,' said Joel.

'And how are you keeping, Ezinna?' he said, watching her with his keen old eyes.

'Grand,' she said, and heard herself say it. Maybe it wasn't so hard to sound 'Cork' after all.

'That's a fine plant,' he said. 'Beautiful flowers. I only noticed it there recently.'

'It's my Mam's,' said Joel.

Ezinna was still holding the empty water bottle in her hand. Suddenly, she felt afraid. It had not struck her until now that planting a tree in a green space that does not belong to you might be a crime — and she wondered what might happen if it was.

'So that's where it came from,' said Deckie.

Ezinna's heart sank. There was no point in denying the facts, not with this old man. 'It grew too big for its pot,' she said. 'And the earth in our back garden is covered in concrete. Will I get into trouble for planting it here?'

'Technically, it's against regulations,' said Deckie. 'But I wouldn't worry about it if I were you. No one will take a tack of notice.'

Ezinna began to worry all the same.

In Nigeria, Ezinna and Obi had been prosperous. They had a car, a house and savings. But all their savings had long gone, to pay the traffickers to take them to England. While they travelled, they kept their documents hidden in their shoes and their passports sewn inside their clothing. When they reached their destination, they took their papers out and begged the person who interviewed them to copy them but not to take the originals away. Much to their confusion, they discovered that they were not in England but in Ireland.

The details about why they left their own country were kept in files in a solicitor's office and in the records of the Refugee Appeals Tribunal and in the paperwork that she and Obi kept safely with them, no matter where they went. They seldom spoke to anyone except the relevant authorities about the corruption that Obi had uncovered, about his refusal to be quiet, about the threats to his life, about the terror they had endured. They rarely spoke, even to each other, about Obi's brother Dele, who had been shot and killed right on their doorstep. He had looked so much – too much – like Obi. Instead, they did their best to understand what they needed to do and followed all the advice they were given. Finally, their appeal was heard and they were granted refugee status. It was one of their happiest days.

The day that she and Obi and the children attended the Citizenship Ceremony in Killarney was also a great day.

There were so many happy people there; Nigerian, Polish, Romanian, Indian and even English, the last of which surprised her. Mr Brian McMahon welcomed them all and administered the Oath of Fidelity and Loyalty. 'You, our newest citizens, should never forget where you came from or erase memories — these will form part of your grandchildren's legacy too,' he said. Ezinna had wept a little, from joy and relief. Then they had taken the bus all the way back home and celebrated with fried chicken and jollof rice and cake.

But a few days later, when the euphoria had worn off, Ezinna gazed at Obi across the table and realised she felt lonely and resentful. She had withstood it all; the terror back home, the limbo of their journey, the sleepless nights, humiliating slights, the purgatory of living in Direct Provision and the waiting, waiting, waiting. She knew she should be grateful, that she should thank the Lord for taking care of them. But what she felt, now that the danger of being sent home was gone, was an awful emptiness; a distance between herself and Obi because the terror was in the past and there was nothing else but living to worry about.

All through that summer, while Obi was at work, when little Blessing was asleep and while Joel watched TV, Ezinna crept across the street to the park to water her little tree. She would look around her carefully before she did so.

'How are you, my little tree?' she would whisper, and the leaves would whisper back.

'Me, I am a little sad today,' she would confide, and the tree would shiver a little in the wind, to show her that it cared. She worried still that someone from the City Council would notice her little tree and make enquiries. Perhaps they would come along and cut it down. At least it was no longer flowering, so it did not stand out as much. Obi had hardly noticed its absence and had not asked where it had gone, so she kept her trouble to herself.

Obi became more and more convinced that another waiter was stealing from the tip jar and perhaps even from the till. Ezinna pleaded with him to say nothing — at least until he had some proof. Who knew what trouble might come to them if he spoke up about such a thing? She had once admired her husband's abilities but now he made her so anxious she could hardly breathe.

Colder days came. Ezinna worried that her tree would die. But the winter turned out to be mild and the tree survived.

Spring came. Some of the people who lived on the terrace now said hello to Ezinna as they passed her by, and some did not. Little Miss O'Neill said that Blessing was indeed a blessing and that Joel was a delightful boy. Some of the parents who waited outside the school greeted her when she and Blessing waited for Joel, and some did not. Marie visited Ezinna to see how she had settled in. 'You should call in to the Cork Migrant Centre,' she said. 'You might make some friends.' Ezinna said she'd think about it. Her little tree began to bloom.

Then the pandemic came.

When the country went into Lockdown and the Covid-19 pandemic swept across the world, Ezinna began to feel as if she was living in a different kind of Direct Provision, where yet again the outcome was uncertain and the end date was unknown.

Obi spent his days slouched on the sitting-room couch, watching daytime TV. Though he had been granted a pandemic allowance, he worried about how long it would last and if he'd ever get his job back. Otherwise he hardly spoke. Blessing toddled round the house, demanding cartoons and cake, or begging Ezinna to take her to the playground.

If Mr O' Toole had not called to the door with a laptop, things would have been even worse. 'It's an old one I had lying around,' he'd said. 'Joel's a bright boy and it wouldn't do for him to fall behind with his schoolwork.' Joel had grinned and said 'Thanks a million, Deckie.' Ezinna and Obi had written a formal letter of thanks.

The death toll rose. The news was bad. The news was worse. They stayed at home and stayed inside and Ezinna cooked and cleaned and washed and scrubbed and FaceTimed her sister in Kaduna and lay awake at night and scarcely left the house except to shop for food. Sometimes, when she was sick and tired of everything, she strode out to the park to tell her fears and worries to her little tree.

One afternoon Ezinna put her jacket on and shoved her purse in her pocket, along with her facemask. Joel was doing what she hoped was homework on the computer but she could not even be bothered to check. She popped her head into the sitting room. Obi was lounging on the couch, watching *Midsomer Murders* on TV. Blessing lay beside him, fast asleep, her pink rabbit clutched in her hands. As Ezinna left the house, she felt cheated by the world. Obi had been strong and smart when she met him, handsome in his uniform, and when trouble came he had been valiant in his determination to find refuge for his family. Now he hardly budged except to search for the TV remote. Joel often gave her cheek and Blessing was like a wind-up toy, except when she was asleep.

Ezinna marched outside, and crossed the street to the little green park, where her little tree, covered in red blossoms, was the only spot of brightness. To her annoyance, a young woman was already right beside it. The woman looked around in a furtive manner that seemed to indicate some sinister intent, and then bent down, as if examining the foliage. Ezinna wondered if it could be someone from the City Council, come to check what kind of tree it was, but surely the people in the Council had better things to do during a pandemic? She took her facemask out and put it on. She walked across the grass in a casual kind of way, as if she were only out for a stroll. When she drew nearer she saw, to her horror, that the young woman was cutting pieces off the lower branches with a pair of secateurs.

My tree, my tree, my tree. It was more than Ezinna could bear. 'What are you doing to this tree?' she demanded. Her own aggressive tone almost shocked her, but it was too late now.

The woman stopped what she was doing and looked up. 'What business is it of yours?' she said.

'This is *my* tree.' Armoured by unhappiness, Ezinna knew she sounded nasty, but she had to stand her ground.

'How can it be your tree? This is a public space.'

'Are you from the Council?'

'No, I'm not.'

'Well then,' said Ezinna, 'Why are you vandalizing this tree?'

The woman put the bits she'd cut off Ezinna's tree carefully on the grass and stood up. 'I was only taking cuttings.'

Ezinna recognised the woman now. She lived in one of the two big houses at the edge of the park. She had a big garden and a whole house to herself.

'It isn't fair,' she heard herself say, but now she sounded sad and a bit envious. 'You have your own garden and your own trees. This is my only tree and you are cutting it.'

'Oh heck,' the woman said. 'I can't do a thing right today.' She threw the secateurs down on the grass and looked as if she was going to cry. 'Look, I don't know what your problem is. It's not your tree. It's not as if I'm stealing anything. Anyway I'm not even sure the cuttings will work. Really, cuttings should be taken early in the morning—but I can't seem to get out of bed these days til noon. I'm so fed up of being alone in the house. I can't seem to write or do anything at all. I think I'm going bonkers.'

Ezinna realised that this was not an evil person, but a woman with troubles of her own.

'Cuttings? What do you mean?' she asked.

'These little strips I've cut off, I'm going to plant them in pots and hopefully they'll grow into fine big shrubs like this one,' the woman said. 'Look, I think we got off to a bad start here. My name's Laura O'Leary. I can give you some plants if the cuttings work out. Would that solve your problem?'

'My name is Ezinna. But I have nowhere to grow my tree.'

Laura looked across at Liberty Terrace. 'You live in Number 3, don't you? I like the orange colour you put on your front door,' she said. 'Don't you have a back garden?'

Ezinna explained that her yard was covered in concrete, that only a few tufts of grass grew between the cracks. That, she confided, was why she had to plant her tree in the park.

'I know your landlord, Gustie Murphy. He's a lazy skinflint, but he's not the worst. I'll ring him and ask if we can hack up the concrete, make it into a proper garden.'

Laura took out her phone and strode away while she was speaking into it. When she returned, she was smiling. 'That's grand, he says, so long as he doesn't have to do anything.' She picked up the cuttings and her secateurs from the ground where she had left them. 'Come over to my house and I'll find some tools.'

Ezinna waited on the footpath outside Laura's gate. She could hear scraping sounds from the open door of Laura's garage. It sounded like furniture being moved. Laura emerged with a pickaxe and a big shovel. 'These belonged to my Dad,' she said, hauling them down the path. 'I'll have another look later on. I can give you everything you'll need.'

Ezinna walked home along the footpath, lugging the pickaxe and shovel across her shoulder. She walked into the hallway and past Joel in the dining room and out into the kitchen and through the back door into the grey backyard. She leaned the shovel against the wall. She grasped the pickaxe with both hands. She took a deep breath and raised it as high as she could and thumped it down on the concrete. The concrete cracked a little, so she tried again and the crack got larger. Then she propped the pickaxe against the dustbin and prised the broken shards of concrete up with the shovel, as Laura had advised. Underneath, the soil looked good and brown. She put the shovel down and took the pickaxe up again. She swung it down and splintered another bit of ageing concrete. It was only a thin layer, after all. She stopped a moment to catch her breath.

'Wow!' said Joel. He was standing in the open kitchen doorway.

'Stay back,' she said. 'I don't want any bits to hit you. But you can help later on, if you want.'

'Okay.' He ran inside. She raised the pickaxe again as high as she could, and thumped it down once more.

'Oh my Lord,' she heard Obi say. He was standing in the doorway and he was smiling. 'You are the strongest woman I know.'

'The landlord has said yes,' she said hurriedly. 'I will have a garden. I have met someone who will lend me all I need.'

Obi took the pickaxe in his hands and motioned her aside. 'I will help you,' he said. He held the pickaxe in his hands for a moment, assessing its heft, and then he swung it back, high above his shoulder, brought it forward in an arc and slammed it down. The pickaxe landed on the concrete with a resounding whack.

'Oh my,' he said as he looked down at the broken shards. 'This feels very, very good.'

Ezinna had forgotten how strong he was. So, she thought, had he.

When Obi turned to smile at her again, she felt like singing.

HUMAN SOUP

It was supposed to take only an hour to get to the faith healer's place but we'd been on the road for an hour and a half. I was annoyed at myself, dying for a cigarette and wondering why on earth I'd let my two neighbours persuade me to drive them. I hadn't a notion of paying out good money to the chancer myself, whether he was the seventh son of a seventh son or not.

Nora O'Neill suffered from car sickness, so she was ensconced in the front passenger seat, propped up with the two car cushions she always brought for extra comfort. She and Betty Healy had refused to wear their facemasks in the car. I wore mine anyway.

'I'm starving,' she said now. 'It's past time I took my pills.'

It wasn't even midday yet and I had no appetite at all, but I forced myself to stay calm.

'Look, there's the sign for Ballyboy,' Betty said from the back seat. 'We could stop for a bite to eat there.'

'Oh, thanks be to the Good Lord Jesus,' said Nora. It was

never a plain Thank God with her. My daughter Frankie nick-named her Nora Kneel and Pray when she was in her teens. Back then, Frankie often made me laugh. These days, she was breaking my heart.

Ballyboy was little more than one street with a few buildings on either side, so it was easy enough to park. I got out of the car and went around to the passenger side to help Nora out. Betty managed to haul herself out of the back seat and she held Nora's arm while I found her walking stick. Once Nora had stabilised herself, they began to amble slow as snails down the street. I lagged behind, my facemask dangling from my wrist, smoking a cigarette.

Nora stopped and half-turned. 'I thought you gave up the fags?' she said.

I ignored her. Why the hell shouldn't I have the odd cig-arette? I'm fifty-nine and the only thing wrong with me is stress. Nora is in her eighties and she never smoked or drank in her life, but she always has about a million different things wrong with her. It was Nora's idea to visit the faith healer, because it was so difficult these days to get a doctor's appointment.

'My rheumatism is killing me,' she had said. 'And I'm getting desperate migraine. Deckie Google says the fella's a wonder.'

Nora and Betty were always mad for road, especially since they'd had to stay inside so much during Lockdown. Now that the travel restrictions had been eased, they were determined to have an outing. I'd gotten used to doing everything for them during the pandemic and, in fairness, they were easy enough to please. Even so, I could tell that Ballyboy was a bit of a let-down. The non-essential shops were shut, which was just as well, because I knew from past experience that Betty's sloth-like approach to shopping could slow the whole day down drastically. There was no hotel, either, only an Indian restaurant, a fish and chip shop and a couple of cafes.

'Fried food is deadly for my diverticulosis,' said Nora as we passed the socially-distanced queue outside The Battered Plaice.

She and Betty straggled across the street to inspect The Olive Branch. I followed in their wake and kept my mouth shut, knowing that any contribution to their laborious decision-making would only complicate the process.

'I'm not sure about it,' Betty said.

Nora was dubious about the Olive Branch too. 'My late husband Finbar, God rest his soul, would never go anywhere to eat except a hotel,' she said. 'He was very pernickety.'

They meandered up the street like penguins on the loose, until finally, we stood outside a place called The Good Egg Café.

'It looks alright. There's lots of stuff that isn't eggs,' said Betty, staring at the menu in the window.

'It'll do,' I said.

Obediently, we put our masks on and sanitized our hands, then waited to be seated. A streelish young girl with long black hair streaked with purple slouched over. She wore a dirty white apron with 'The Good Egg Cafe' printed on it, above a smiley-faced yellow egg, and her disposable facemask was slipping off her nose.

'Here or takeaway?' she said.

'Here,' I said, and she nodded us to a table near the window.

'Do you do half-portions?' Nora asked.

'We don't,' said the girl, pushing her mask back over her

nose.

'What's your soup of the day?'

'Keratinhummin,' the girl said, taking a pencil and pad out of her apron pocket.

'Excuse me,' said Nora. 'Could you repeat that?'

'Carrot 'n human.' The girl spoke a little slower this time.

'Carrot and Human?' Nora stared at the waitress. 'Sorry, what was the second thing?'

'Cumin,' the girl said.

'Oh, cumin,' I said. 'The spice, she means the spice, Nora. Cumin, not human.'

Nora looked at me, her bright little eyes peering above her mask, and the penny dropped. She started chuckling and Betty joined in. In seconds they were laughing like hyenas, fit to burst.

'I thought I was going mental,' spluttered Nora, wiping her eyes. 'I was imagining a big black cauldron with limbs sticking up out of it and cannibals with spears dancing around.'

'Me too,' said Betty. 'Like in *The Beano* or *The Dandy*, those comics we used have long ago.'

The waitress looked through the window as she tapped her pencil on her pad. 'Em, I'll come back later, when you've decided,' she said.

'No. We'll order now,' I said. If I could have slapped her snooty little face, I would have. I was in no mood for cheek from young ones. I'd had enough of that last night from Frankie.

Betty pulled herself together first. 'I'll have the soup,' she said.

'And me,' said Nora. 'I can't resist the thought of it.'

'I'll have the same.' I said.

The waitress raised her eyebrows and scribbled on her notepad before she turned away.

'Finbar would have gone crazy if he was with us. He'd

have given out stink about the service,' said Nora. 'God rest his soul and the souls of all the Departed.'

'Bill wouldn't be with us at all,' said Betty. 'He was always in the pub.'

And worse, I thought. Bill Healy was dead five years or more, but it was common knowledge that he'd been no angel. Thank goodness Betty never knew about his shenanigans — or maybe she pretended that she didn't. My daughter Frankie used to call him 'Sexual Healy' after the Marvin Gaye song — but, oh, I forced myself not to think about Frankie and how she'd changed since then.

'She's a right little miss, that waitress,' I said.

'Ah, those uppity young ones are a pain in the neck,' said Nora. 'But it gave me a laugh, so it did.'

The waitress came back and plonked brown bread and soup on the table. We took our masks off and began to eat.

'How's Frankie doing?' asked Nora. She was busy rubbing the last of her bread around the inside of her soup bowl. 'She must be fed up of being stuck at home.'

'They're fine,' I said. I hesitated, waiting for a reaction but none came. 'We're fine,' I added.

'It was hard on you when Richard died so young,' said Betty. 'But you did a great job with her, Martha, in fairness to you.'

I didn't want to think about Richard either, about how much I missed him now, about all those years together, about our longing for a baby, about how we'd almost given up hope, and then the miracle, the shock of it, the magic I had felt when first I held that tiny bundle in my arms, about how happy we were then.

Instead, I wiped my mouth with my paper napkin.

'That soup wasn't bad,' I said.

'Sure my Great Auntie Dot was one a'them carbon

neutrals,' said Nora, as she put her pillbox on the table. 'They used to say she had a kind of a stump...'

Betty interrupted. 'How about tea?' she said. She stood up and shoved her mask back on. 'I'll go up and order some.'

'Yes, please,' I said.

Nora said she'd have some too.

Betty came back to the table holding three small forks and a slice of cake on a plate.

'Madeira cake,' she said. 'I thought we could share.'

It took ages for the tea to arrive. We had to ask the waitress twice for milk. When it came, Nora stirred the teapot and poured with a shaky hand. I added milk to mine and stirred.

Betty coughed and looked at me. 'I can never understand why people are the way they are, but I suppose we just have to make the best of things.' She sliced the cake into three. No one said a word for a few minutes while we ate and drank.

Then I broke the silence. 'I think it's time to head off,' I said.

Nora's pet widower, Deckie Google, had written down the directions from Ballyboy in careful blue biro on the back of an envelope but Nora made a right mess of the navigation and I missed the turn-off twice.

'You could do with a sat nav around these parts,' said Betty, from her perch in the back. That was rich, coming from her. Betty could hardly use her own mobile phone.

At last, I turned into the narrow boreen and drove slowly onwards.

'It's definitely down here,' Nora said, her voice high and nervous.

The bushes and nettles and briars of the ditches along the sides of the road leaned in towards the car as if they wanted rid of us and the car bounced up and down in the lane. My bra felt uncomfortably tight, the back of my neck was beginning to ache and I worried how I would manage if a car happened to come in the opposite direction, for the passing places were few and far between.

'Thanks be to the Good Lord Jesus,' said Nora when we spotted the farmhouse at the end of the lane.

A large farmyard surrounded the whitewashed two-storey house, and an empty barn stood beside it. About a dozen cars and three horseboxes were already parked in the front yard but there was just about enough room to park outside the front door. As I hauled myself out of the car, I could see a young man trying with only limited success to drag a nervy chestnut brown horse around the side of the house.

The front door was open and a sign sellotaped in the window next to it read:

MURTY LANE - HEALER
Mondays and Thursdays only: 10 a.m. – 3 p.m.
Horses €50
Clients €30
Dogs €20
FACEMASKS MUST BE WORN INDOORS.

'Why don't ye go in and check it out,' I said to the ladies. 'I'll see you in a minute.'

'She's going to have another one of those dirty fags,' Nora mumbled to Betty as they shambled off. I felt like screaming but I didn't.

Instead, I walked around the side of the house to look for somewhere quiet to smoke. Behind the house, a row of stables lay across a cobbled yard, where the young fella was trying to calm down the jittery horse, barely managing to hold onto its bridle as it stamped and whinnied and clacked its hooves on the cobblestones.

Next to the back door of the house was a long wooden bench so I went over to it, sat down and took my cigarettes and lighter out of my bag.

An older man, lean and tanned, around my own age, emerged from the back door and approached the horse slowly. He began to stroke the horse, talking to it in a low voice and it whinnied once at him and then calmed down.

As I was lighting up, a big-boned girl in jeans and a short-sleeved t-shirt came around the corner. An elderly golden Labrador limped along behind her. The dog wasn't on a lead, but he was so slow he didn't need one. The girl walked over to the bench and sat down carefully at the end farthest away from me. Both of her arms were tattooed with a line of small butterflies in blues and pinks and yellows and her hair was the same rich colour as the dog's. I was fairly sure she was a girl and not a fella, but I was learning to be cautious about that kind of thing. The Labrador slumped down heavily on the ground next to her, as if he was glad to have a break. The girl took a bright blue vape out of her pocket and inhaled. She blew out a massive cloud of smoke, then leaned down to pat the dog.

'Good boy,' she said. 'Good boy.'

The dog smiled up at her, the way Labradors do, before stretching out for a nap. She sucked the vape again, then blew another cloud of chemicals out in front of her.

'Do you prefer it to the real thing?' I asked her.

'The vape? Well, it took a bit of getting used to, but it's much cheaper than cigarettes,' she said.

'I gave up for years,' I said, taking another drag from my cigarette, 'but with all the stress of the past while, I started smoking again and now I'm like a chimney.'

'Vaping is better,' she said. 'I honestly don't miss the

cigarettes now.'

We sat there inhaling our different forms of dirty old smoke and watching the older man as he patted the chestnut horse and whispered to him gently. The young lad stood back, the reins loose now in his hands.

'That older man. He's the healer, is he?'

'Yeah, that's Murty. I love the way he deals with animals,' she said.

The healer moved in front of the horse and stared into his eyes and kept talking, and the horse lowered his head and nudged him, as if to ask for a caress. The healer rubbed the animal's forehead, then slowly moved around him, patting him gently, all along his body and up and down his haunches. When he checked the hooves, the horse lifted each hoof as if he knew what to do even before he was asked. The healer kept on talking and stroking him. It was mesmerising to watch.

'He always does the horses first,' the girl said. 'Then the dogs. He does the humans last, first come first served.'

'What's wrong with your own dog?'

'Poor old Lucky. He's my parents' dog really, but I love him. He's getting old and his bones ache, so he suffers from depression. Since I've been bringing him to Murty, though, he's perked up a lot.'

Everyone's depressed now, even the dogs. No such thing as put up and shut up nowadays. Even before this damn Covid, everyone wanted to have their cake and eat it and if one cake didn't suit them they wanted a different one. I didn't say that though. I took another drag of my cigarette instead. I'd taken a shine to the girl because, in spite of the tattoos, she seemed nice and normal. I liked the way she looked at the old dog, and the way he looked back up at her with his big Labrador smile.

'Did it hurt much to have those tattoos done?' I asked because it was nice sitting there, having a chat with a stranger, outside my own four walls, for a change.

'Not really,' she said. 'It's a nice addictive kind of pain. My first one was the most painful, but it was worth it. I'll show you.' She dragged her t-shirt down over one shoulder to expose her shoulder blade. The tattoo, an intricately formed pink rose, with a green stem and sharp red thorns, was pretty, like something a little girl would choose. Not like the ugly ones Frankie turned up with when she came back from college.

The girl pushed her t-shirt back up. 'Sorry,' she said. 'You're probably not a tattoo-type person.'

'No, it's very nice,' I said, but she was right. I had no idea why people wanted tattoos in the first place, and why anyone would be willing to go through all that pain to get them.

'You'll feel great after you see Murty,' she said.

'I'm not going to see him at all.'

She looked at me in surprise.

'My neighbours asked me to bring them,' I said. 'That's the only reason I'm here.' I stubbed out my fag and put it in my pocket. Then I walked around to the front of the house, put my mask back on and went inside.

A sellotaped sign on a door in the hall said 'Bathroom', so I went in, put my fag end in the bin and went to the loo. I washed my hands, and sanitised them afterwards for good measure. Then I went through the door marked 'Waiting Room', where the first thing I noticed was a framed poster of Elvis Presley — as a young lad, with his guitar — on the far wall. Next to it was a statue of the Virgin Mary on a wooden stand. About ten people were sitting on mismatched chairs placed as far away from each other as the room allowed. A door in the far wall was marked 'Meeting Room'. Betty and Nora were sitting together on a sagging couch in the corner, masked up like elderly bandits. Betty waved me over and shoved closer to Nora to make space for me. I sat down and closed my eyes and tried to get Frankie out of my mind.

I must have nodded off because all of a sudden Betty was tapping me on the shoulder.

'Go on,' she said. 'You're next. I paid for you already.'

'What?' I said, still half-asleep.

'Get up,' she hissed. 'He's waiting for you.'

I stood up automatically and she shoved me forward towards the door marked 'Meeting Room' that Nora was limping out of.

'Go on in,' said Betty, and everyone else in the room seemed to look up, as if annoyed that I was delaying them. Before I rightly knew what I was doing, I found myself walking towards the door and stepping inside.

The healer was washing his hands at a small white sink in the corner. He turned around and his eyes looked wise above his mask.

'You're very welcome. Take a seat,' he said, indicating a solitary bentwood chair in the middle of the room.

I blinked a couple of times and stood there, staring at the chair, wondering how on earth I'd managed to get myself into this situation.

'You're here with the other two ladies from Cork City,' he said. 'Are you a widow too?'

'I am. But I'm only their chauffeur. I didn't intend to come in at all.'

'That's alright, Martha,' he said. 'But since you're here, why don't you sit down for a minute?'

Reluctantly, I sat on the chair and he stood opposite me, keeping his distance.

'Your friends told me how kind you are, and how much they value your support,' he said.

'That's very nice of them,' I said. 'But I don't wish to avail of your services.' I nearly told him I didn't believe in that kind of mumbo jumbo, but I didn't like to be rude.

'I wouldn't want to put you under any pressure,' he said. 'I'll give you back the contribution they gave me.' I felt embarrassed. Maybe he wasn't a complete chancer after all. And I'd seen him with the horse.

'Look, sure, keep the money and go ahead, so,' I said. I'd get the thing over and done with, and it would be easier to deal with Betty and Nora than if I refused.

He stepped behind me and I flinched slightly as he laid his hands on my shoulders. The room was very quiet. All I could feel were his warm steady hands pressing gently down on me and all I could hear was the ticking of a clock and my own heartbeat, until he began to chant some low repetitive prayer. Marantha. Come, Oh Lord. As he prayed, I closed my eyes and felt intense heat surging from his hands into my flesh, like the rush that comes from opening a hot oven, or the steam that rises when a lid is lifted from a boiling pot. A wave of utter sorrow washed over me and tears began to slide down from the edges of my eyes onto the fabric of my mask. The more I tried to stop myself, the more I wept, shuddering with grief beneath the steady hands that held my shoulders.

My daughter hates me. Once I had Richard and our beautiful little girl, and an ordinary kind of happiness. Now there's only me and Frankie stuck at home during a pandemic and she's not the person she used to be, and she despises me.

While I was thinking all that and weeping into my mask, the healer continued chanting prayers to a God I don't believe in until I finally calmed down. Then he handed me a box of tissues. I wiped my eyes and told him about Frankie.

'She cut off her beautiful hair,' I said. 'She wears what they call a binder. She says she was born in the wrong body. She's cross with me all the time. I forget to call her 'they' and it drives her berserk. I can't understand it. Maybe I'm not trying enough.'

What I didn't tell him was that it had all come to a head the night before.

The evening had gone better than expected. I'd cooked a vegetarian lasagne, Frankie's favourite. Then I watched *The Crown* on Netflix, while Frankie was upstairs on her computer.

I'd left the renewal papers for our Laya Health Insurance on the kitchen table. God knows I had been glad of the private health cover when Richard got sick, but it was terribly expensive, so I was planning on ringing them in the morning to see if I could get a discount.

Later on, when I went into the kitchen to boil the kettle for a cup of tea, I found Frankie sitting at the table studying the paperwork. When she looked up and stared at me, I knew we were in trouble.

'This health insurance is no use,' she said. 'We need to change it.'

'Why? What's wrong with it?'

'It doesn't cover gender reassignment.'

I tried to stay calm. 'Does that matter?'

'Of course it does.' She picked up the insurance policy and threw it on the floor, where it landed like a slap. 'I might have known you'd say that. You're determined not to support me.'

'Look, I don't care if you're gay or straight or bi or whatever.' I knew I was saying the wrong thing, but I simply couldn't stop. 'But to have an unnecessary and painful operation... I think it's pure madness.'

'You don't have a bloody clue, TERF.' She looked at me as if I was dirt. 'You understand nothing.'

And then, I lost it. 'The cheek of you,' I said. 'How dare you call me a TERF! Don't tell me I haven't a clue. I've stood up for human rights all my life. I've voted for the Eighth Amendment, for marriage equality, went on anti-nuke marches before you were born...'

But she stomped upstairs to her room before I'd finished speaking. As the kettle whistled itself to a halt, I felt that something between myself and Frankie had been broken beyond repair. She was still in bed when I left the house the next morning.

It was time to get on the road again. Nora adjusted her cushions in the front passenger seat before she sat in. I looked around to make sure Betty had hauled herself in and closed the door. Then I put the car into gear and drove slowly back down the narrow boreen.

'He looked a bit like Dickie Rock, didn't he?' said Betty approvingly. 'How did you get on, Nora?'

'Grand,' said Nora. 'I could swear I'm already feeling better. He says I need to stop worrying and that will help the migraine. But the old bones are feeling better already.'

'That's good,' said Betty. 'I wish Deckie Google told me he didn't do eczema, but I'm glad I went, all the same. How about you Martha?'

'I'm alright, thanks,' I said.

We were almost home. I drove slowly up Hope Street and turned into Liberty Terrace. I stopped the car outside Nora's house. She was curled up asleep in the front, little whistling snorts coming from her. I shook her gently awake. She looked a little dishevelled, but she was smiling all the same.

'I haven't had so much fun in ages,' she said. 'We should go on another outing soon.'

'Good idea,' said Betty from the back seat.

'I'll consult with Decky Google,' said Nora. 'He can check to see what's open.'

As I was taking Nora's walking stick out of the boot, Deckie Google came down the street as if he'd been expecting us. He was looking dapper as usual, in a three-piece suit with matching tie and facemask.

'I'll see Mrs. O'Neill safely in,' he said. He helped Nora to extricate herself from the front seat and held her steady until she had her walking stick safely in her little hand. As she thanked me for the outing, he tucked her cushions under one arm and took her elbow in the other. I watched as he escorted her to her front door. Deckie might be a know-it-all, I thought, but he was a gentleman through and through.

'Thank you, Martha,' Betty said. Her face looked grey and tired. She fumbled in her pocket, fished out two fivers and thrust them at me. 'That's from us, towards the petrol.'

I protested but she pushed my hand away. I watched her walk slowly up the path towards her own front door. I kept watching until the door closed behind her.

The house seemed awful quiet when I went in. I hung up my coat and threw the car keys into the bowl. A pile of shredded paper lay on the kitchen table. The Health Insurance documents had been torn into tiny pieces.

I walked back into the hallway.

'Frankie,' I called, but there was no reply.

I walked slowly upstairs. Frankie's bedroom door was open. My child was sitting at the desk, staring at the computer screen.

'Frankie,' I said.

My child said nothing. The failure to turn around and the tapping of the keys on the keyboard clearly signified rejection.

I stared at the back of that familiar head, the stubborn set of that rigid spine, the curve of those delicate shoulder blades, and I could not, would not, did not turn away.

Instead, I walked towards my child and laid my hands, gently, on those beloved shoulders. I kept my hands there, firm and steady, hoping they felt warm, and I prayed, in my own way, for something, anything, even the smallest of miracles.

DECKIE GOOGLE

Deckie Google is returning from his afternoon perambulation when he sees Martha's car pulling up outside Nora O'Neill's house. He automatically adjusts his tie and pats the pocket of his jacket to check that a triangle of matching handkerchief is showing. He pats the mask on his face to make sure it still covers his nose. A former senior Garda, he's no slouch. Though he retired ten years and seven months ago, he's determined to maintain his standards.

He walks towards the car as Martha gets out of the driver's seat. Nora is in the front passenger seat and Betty Healy is sitting in the back. Martha, the only one wearing a mask, is the first to see him.

'Hello Deckie,' she says as she opens the boot of the car and takes out Nora's walking stick.

'You made good time,' he says. Martha is so competent, he thinks, but then she's a lot younger than the others. Late fifties, maybe, he thinks, or early sixties, but it's hard to tell. She's not the kind that would tell you herself and he suspects she dyes her hair.

'We're just back from the faith healer,' Martha tells him. 'Nora fell asleep on the way home. She's only just after waking up.'

He peers through the window of the front passenger seat. Sweet, diminutive Nora O'Neill's eyes twinkle as she waves at him through the glass. She's wearing a knitted hat that reminds him of a raspberry and a multi-coloured scarf wound loosely round her neck, right up to her chin.

'May I assist your ladyship?' he says as he opens her car door.

Nora edges sideways on her seat until her feet are dangling out of the car and he gently grasps her hands to tow her slowly out and upwards, as he always does. Once she's safely vertical on the footpath, he holds her elbow to keep her balanced.

'Well, we made it there and back, thanks be to the Good Lord Jesus,' she says.

Betty is unwinding herself out of the back seat of the car.

'Declan,' she says. 'Good to see you.'

She stands up slowly on the path, massaging her lower back with one hand, then stretching both hands in the air for a moment. Betty, he thinks to himself, is a fine figure of a woman for her age. Always nicely turned out, like Nora, but better-preserved, truth be told. Nora is far more fun, though, despite her apparent religiosity.

Martha is beside him now. She passes the walking stick to Nora, and once Nora has a firm grasp of it, Declan releases her elbow. Nora's getting very shaky on the pins, he thinks, but he mustn't overdo it. She needs the bit of dignity.

Martha leans into the front passenger seat and emerges with two familiar cushions, embroidered with unnatural birds. Nora insists on bringing them with her whenever Deckie takes her for a drive. 'I need the padding,' she always says. 'It's desperate when you have hardly any flesh on the old bones.' Thankfully, she makes it sound more like a private joke than a painful truth.

'I'll take those for you,' he offers. 'And I'll see Mrs O'Neill safely in.'

'Ever the gentleman,' Nora says.

Martha hands him Nora's cushions and he tucks them both under one arm.

Nora tilts her head, birdlike, towards Martha. 'Thank you again, Martha, for doing all that driving.'

Deckie, formerly known as Chief Superintendent Declan O'Toole, was somewhat miffed at first when he found out that the ladies were going on the outing without him. After all, he's in a support bubble with Nora and Betty. He's the one who always drove them to Mass, until they had to make do with watching it on TV. He's also the one who researched the faith healer Nora had heard about, checked out the fellow's credentials online, did an unofficial Garda vetting and figured out their itinerary. But when Nora explained to him that she and Betty thought Martha needed a bit of healing, and that they'd never persuade her to go unless they made out they needed her to drive them, he calmed down.

'May the Good Lord forgive me. I told her you didn't want to go on account of the risks,' Nora said. 'But it was only a white lie.'

Deckie agreed. Anyway, he can never be cross with Nora for long. He always sees in her mischievous little eyes the merry young girl she must have been in her youth. It was Nora who started calling him Deckie Google, and the others had followed suit. He'd never had a nickname until he moved to Liberty Terrace and he was surprised to find he didn't mind it.

Sometimes he wishes that he'd met Nora when they were young, for she is such good company and her sense of humour always cheers him. It's a platonic relationship, of course. One marriage had been enough for him. Delia passed away from cancer in 1994 and their marriage had been far from perfect, though neither of them ever dared admit it. Thank goodness, Nora's far more interested in a bit of gossip and a cup of tea.

'Did ye have a good time?' he asks Nora as he opens her garden gate.

'We did, thank God,' she says. 'And we managed to get Martha in to have a session with the healer, in spite of herself.'

Nora fumbles in her shoulder bag for her keys. Her hand trembles as she tries to put the key in her front door and Deckie has to stop himself from taking it out of her hand and opening the door himself. A touch of Parkinsons, he suspects. He wonders if his own tremor is as bad as hers. He would like to invite her to his house for supper—he has two of those Lidl fish and chip suppers in the freezer and really they're very good—but he can see that she is tired, so he probably should refuse even the obligatory cup of tea.

The key clicks in the lock and the door swings inwards. He's glad he oiled the lock for her last month, when he'd noticed how she struggled with it.

Nora's kitchen table is covered with a wipe-clean floral table cloth. A pack of disposable face masks lies there, next to the usual array — a lidded sugar bowl painted with a red dragon and the words *A Souvenir of Wales*, her Wedgewood salt and pepper pots, a red cast iron teapot trivet, a bowl of rosy apples with wizened skin and yesterday's *Examiner*.

He puts the cushions on a chair as she limps towards the kettle and switches it on.

'You'll have a cup of tea?' she says. 'I need to ask you something.'

'Just a quick cup,' he says.

'So was the trip a success?' he says.

'It's hard to know for sure,' she says. 'I don't think Martha's in good form and I'm not sure how to help her.'

'Is she under the weather or what?' Deckie is puzzled. He has grown to like Martha, in spite of her standoffishness. Since March, when the whole pandemic thing kicked off, he and Martha had made certain, sure and positive that the older people living nearby wanted for nothing. Martha is opinionated though. She had tried to force him to cocoon at first, and they had fallen out over that — sure he was fit as a fiddle and only barely seventy — but in the end, he got his way and they'd made a great team. When the country went to Level 3, she had organised a little celebration — socially distanced in her backyard, with tea and cakes and a bottle of fancy wine.

'I figure she's feeling a bit low about Frankie.'

'What's the problem with Frankie?' he says.

'I think she has "issues",' says Nora, carefully.

Now that he thinks about it, he feels sure that Nora is right. The last time he saw Frankie it was hard to tell if she was a girl or a fella. He'd hardly recognised her at first. She looked nothing like the sweet little girl with hair tied in ribbons who used to knock on his door asking for sponsorship for charity walks, years ago. This other

Frankie, this changeling, had fairly reeked of misery. She must be twenty or thereabouts now. He's fairly sure she's finished college but she might be doing the final year online.

'Issues?' Deckie says.

Nora coughs. 'I'd say she doesn't know whether she's coming or going,' she says, staring at her fridge. 'In the sexual sense.'

'Indeed,' says Deckie. He's astounded, not by Nora's words (her forthright observations, leavened by religious invocations, are unusual for a woman of her age but he's grown accustomed to them) but by the fact that she has had to explain what should have been, in retrospect, entirely obvious to him.

The kettle comes to the boil and doesn't seem to have any intention of clicking off. He gets up and tips the switch.

'I'll make it,' he says. He pours boiling water into Nora's teapot, swishes it round and empties it into the sink. He puts three teabags into the pot and fills it up from the kettle. Then he takes it carefully over to the table and places it on the trivet.

'Of course, you can be anything you like these days,' Nora says as she slides digestive biscuits onto a plate. 'I couldn't care less, myself. Sure, even that Phillip Schofield who does the morning show on ITV—he's gay. The Good Lord makes allowances.'

'Indeed,' he says, again.

'Judge not, lest ye be judged, it says in the Bible.' Nora adds, her hand shaking perilously as she pours tea into china cups.

Afterwards, in his own quiet house, Deckie switches his

computer on. He loves his laptop. but the familiar whirring sound it makes as it boots up fails to reassure him in the normal way. After he retired, he did a few computer courses so that he could keep on working on his cold cases. He'd copied the files for himself — crimes from the '80s and '90s, cases he cared about that still disturbed him, the ones that got away. Strictly speaking, he wasn't allowed to keep any paperwork, but some detectives did it, to protect themselves as much as anything else. The internet makes all the difference now. He can scour all kinds of sites for new information and the research keeps his brain in tune.

His computer skills have come in handy during the Pandemic. He already had his online banking organised and his bills on direct debit. He and Martha do a weekly run to the supermarket for neighbours who are cocooning. They take turns going downtown on errands too. They collect prescriptions from the chemist, buy fresh bread and fish from the English Market and pick up little treats. Nora and Betty trust him with their debit cards and pin numbers, and he keeps meticulous accounts, printed out each week, that tally exactly with their bank statements. He googles the Covid-19 statistics every morning too, and shoves A4 pages summarising the news through all the letterboxes in the neighbourhood. Martha says it's hardly necessary, but he feels it's essential for people to get correct information from a reliable source. Anyway, it keeps him busy.

Now, he riffles through a cold case file but cannot concentrate. He thinks of Frankie and her unhappiness, while Nora's words are running around in his head.

'Of course, you can be anything you like these days.'

'The Good Lord makes allowances.'

'Judge not, lest ye be judged.'

He remembers Delia, and how gentle and ladylike she

had been. They had tried to make the best of things, but he suspected she had always known, deep down, that marrying him had been a mistake.

Something else he's pushed to the back of his mind for years is forcing its way into his consciousness. He closes his file, and though he feels a horrible reluctance, he types a name into Google and begins to search. Somehow or other, he must finally make amends.

He was cock of the walk that time. Only twenty-nine and already a Sergeant in the small town of Atharnavar. Not a glamorous posting, as such, and only a four-man station, but still a metropolis compared to the lonely townland where he'd been reared, and he wasn't about to turn his nose up at it. He'd settled in well, met Delia, who was crazy about him, and somehow, between the jigs and the reels, he'd ended up asking her to marry him. Back then, they were mostly happy, some of the time.

Deckie had noticed the young man loitering downtown. A beautiful face, Deckie had thought. All he needed was a decent haircut. He'd stared at him and the lad had looked right back until Deckie was forced to lower his eyes.

O'Malley, the local TD and bible thumper, had an air of supreme confidence — so much so that Deckie always felt intimidated in his presence. The man practically owned the town, but on that particular morning when O'Malley summoned him to his residence, he looked dishevelled and despairing.

'My son Brian,' he said. 'We've tried everything to fix him. I'm appealing to you, Sergeant. I know you can be trusted with this.'

His son was seventeen, his father said, and going to the

bad. The priest had prayed over him non-stop but couldn't get the evil out of him. The doctor had organised a place for him up in a Dublin hospital — a Special Unit where they could cure him — but he was refusing to go. O'Malley was afraid they'd lose the place. 'I don't know who else to turn to,' he said. 'Put him in the squad car. It's the only way we'll get him there.'

The young man was summoned to the sitting room and looked straight into Deckie's eyes. Yet again, Deckie thought how beautiful he was, and looked away.

'Please,' Brian said. 'Help me. Don't listen to my father. They're all mad. There's nothing wrong with me. I don't want to go.'

Mrs O'Malley stood in the hall, white-faced, while Deckie and O'Malley wrestled the young lad out the front door and into the back of the squad car.

'Mam, tell them,' the young man pleaded, but she bowed her head and said nothing.

'It's for your own good,' his father said, as he flung himself into the back seat beside his son and slammed the door. 'Hit the road, Sergeant and don't listen to him.'

'For God's sake, turn around,' Brian said as Deckie drove at top speed out of town. 'You have no right to do this.'

'You can shut your gob,' his father said. 'The Sergeant here has a court order. Isn't that right, Sergeant?'

And in the swelter of the squad car, gripping the sticky steering wheel, those words slipped out too easily. 'That's right', Deckie said. A white lie, he told himself afterwards, and tried to put it out of his mind. Six months later, he was promoted and sent to a station in the city. O'Malley had made sure of that.

Deckie stares at his computer screen. He, the factfinder, the man who keeps meticulous paperwork, who backs up everything with proof, he, the righteous man, who had been unpopular among his fellow Gardaí because he didn't cut corners... he hadn't actually seen any court order.

Afterwards, he'd discovered the only justification for the whole thing was a letter from the parish priest. He should have questioned what was going on. What was the saying? *When good men do nothing.* In his defence, he tells himself that after all he had to uphold the law. You could get ten years to life for being gay in those days. Maybe Brian had been saved a lot of trouble in the long run — but he doubted it. He knew more now than he did then, about attempted exorcisms, conversion therapy, electric shocks. He'd been co-opted into someone else's nightmare. Church and State, trying to knock it out of them.

But surely he's a good man, even still? He's never opened up about his private life, for he owed that much to Delia's memory. Anyway, it was nobody's business but his own. He told himself for years that he could not have done any differently, but now he feels haunted by the need to make amends.

He taps and scrolls and googles, searching for Brian O'Malley from Atharnavar. He'd be fifty-eight or thereabouts now — if he's still alive. Deckie scours the internet, runs an unofficial Garda vetting, checks the electoral lists, searches for the name. He frantically types and taps on his keyboard as if his life depends on it.

Nothing turns up at first, so he starts in on social media. Facebook first. There seem to be hundreds of Brian O'Malleys. He scrolls and clicks and scrolls and clicks. Finally, he thinks he's found the boy. Surprisingly, the page is not protected. Deckie can see all the photos, all the posts. This Brian—

it's him alright — lives in Cornwall and looks tanned and healthy. Deckie investigates the Facebook page and studies all the evidence. Brian runs a garden centre and posts a lot of photographs of plants. His partner is a landscape architect, a slightly younger-looking man. They own a dog, a nice-looking Sheepdog called Ted. They invite friends to dinner; it is clear that they both like to cook. They go sailing. They belong to a book club. They go on long walks and stop for lunch in quaint, old-fashioned pubs. They smile a lot.

Deckie should be relieved. He tells himself that all's well that ends well. But he doesn't feel well. He doesn't feel well at all.

TROLLEY

Bernice, still in pyjamas, stared into her spotless Siemens fridge. All that remained was an almost empty carton of skim milk, an inch of hardened Emmenthal, a plain yogurt, some limp spring onions, half a Cos lettuce yellowed around its frayed edges and a carrot that had seen better days. Someone once told her that if you look in someone's fridge and there's nothing in it, get out of the house fast, because that person is a psychopath. Well, of course she wasn't a psychopath. There was nothing whatsoever wrong with her, though in normal circumstances she could understand how someone might draw some negative conclusions. She was just a woman living alone during a pandemic, with a fridge freezer that was far too large for one person. No one but herself was going to be looking in her fridge any time soon. It was safer that way.

She tugged on the door of the freezer and pulled out each drawer to inspect the contents. All that remained was a small plastic bag of frozen pizza dough left over from Ambrose's pizza-making spree, half a bag of frozen cauliflower tied with a twisty and a couple of trays of ice cubes. She'd worked her way dismally through the organic lamb that Ambrose had bought from O'Flynn's Butchers back in March. The bag of frozen scallops from the English Market was long gone. So were the packs of frozen spinach and peas, the leftover chicken cacciatore, the mint chocolate ice cream he'd made from scratch. She pushed the freezer door shut. She had coped perfectly well, all things considered and had let nothing go to waste.

Still, today was Saturday and she really should stock up at a supermarket. She felt heavy and slow, as if she were swimming through soup. She hated shopping at the best of times. She'd have to queue and wear a mask. Her car hadn't been driven in — what? — three months. It might not even start.

It was 2020 and Lockdown had begun in March. Since then, she'd hardly left the house, apart from an occasional masked foray into the city centre to buy fresh fish and cheese in the English Market or a short walk to the corner shop on Hope Street to buy basics like milk, bread and eggs. She'd survived mainly on pasta with pesto and an occasional toasted cheese sandwich. She'd never been much of a cook and had not eaten anything fancy since those brief halcyon days — those two weekends in March — when Ambrose cooked for her. Just as well, she thought, because if the whole 'Ambrose phase', as she now termed it in her head, had carried on, she'd be as fat as a pig by now.

She looked around at her new kitchen. What had possessed her to spend so much money on it? If it had been up to Ambrose she'd have spent even more. She remembered how he'd been extolling the virtues of a hideously expensive Fisher & Paykel fridge freezer. It's my dream to have one of those, just like on *MasterChef*, he'd said.

Still, the kitchen had turned out well and the timing had,

in retrospect, been perfect. The whole job had been finished two weeks before the Lockdown had begun. Bernice looked with approval at the grey and white fitted cupboards and the marble effect Corian countertop, the six-ring stainless steel gas hob and overhead hood, the 'self-cleaning' electric oven, the coloured Joseph Joseph chopping board set that Sheila and Siobhan from work had given her as a kitchen-warming gift. Wooden spoons stood in a red ceramic utensil holder that picked up the colour of the paint on the far wall, where the new patio doors led out into the small, bedraggled back garden.

The old wooden breadboard lay adrift on the counter like a senior citizen in a swanky wine bar. Next to it sat Ambrose's deep fat fryer. He'd used it the very first time he'd cooked for her. Now she ran her finger along the lid, leaving a streak on the light coating of greasy dust. She'd have to clean it at some stage. She'd have to figure out a way of returning it to him. Maybe he'd bought a new one by now. Well, he hadn't replied to her text, and everyone was working from home — so she wasn't going to let herself worry about it, for now. She sighed and found a piece of paper and a pen, began to check her kitchen cupboards and make a list.

Upstairs, Bernice forced herself to get showered and dressed. Then she looked through her bedroom window at the small green park across the street and rubbed her eyelids. She really needed to go outside, get some fresh air, see what the outside world was like, but her eyeballs felt as if they were about to fall out of their sockets. Too many online meetings. Too much peering at a screen. Too many texts and emails. Too much online Scrabble. Too much obsessive scrolling on Facebook and Twitter. She was tempted to go back to bed but instead she tied her awful too-long hair up in a knot and put some makeup on her pale, sad face.

In the street outside her house, Bernice blinked her eyes and dug her car keys out of her purse. Everything seemed too bright, even though the sky was cloudy. As she threw her shopping bags into the back seat of her car she noticed Deckie Google and tiny Miss O'Neill shuffling towards her along the footpath. Deckie held Nora's arm gently as they walked along. They looked like a pair of elderly soap stars, all dressed up with nowhere to go. Ironic that these oldies — they must be in their eighties — had a better social life than Bernice. Bernice's late mother, Mrs. Callinan, had disliked Deckie — too nosy for his own good — and deemed Nora too sweet to be wholesome. But Bernice had rarely agreed with her mother on anything. The kindness of her neighbours was one of the reasons why she'd stayed in Liberty Terrace after she'd inherited it in 2016. The other reason was that she couldn't figure out what else to do.

Deckie and Nora stopped at a respectable self-distancing distance and smiled at her.

'How are you keeping, Bernice?' said Nora.

'Not too bad,' said Bernice. 'Going to the shops. Do you need anything?'

'No thank you love. Our supply chain is top class,' said Nora.

'Not like it'll be in England when Boris finally delivers Brexit,' said Deckie. He was always up to date on current affairs. 'Between this pandemic and Boris and Trump and everything else we don't know whether we're coming or going.'

'True,' said Bernice.

'But sure if we get as far as Christmas we'll be on the pig's back come the New Year,' said Deckie.

Get as far as Christmas? thought Bernice as she drove

away. It was only June. Surely everything would be back to normal by at least September? Travel restrictions had been eased and she could travel anywhere within the county. She decided to head out to Ballincollig. The Tesco there was clean and spacious, and the car park on the ground floor was free of charge.

Bernice was thirty-nine and divorced. In 2015, at the same time as her marriage was disintegrating, the death of her father hit her hard. The following year, her mother and brother had been killed in a terrorist incident while on a weekend break in Paris, an event so shocking that Bernice felt, for a while, unreal, like an actor in a TV soap. It was ironic, Bernice thought, that as a result of all the tragedies she had no mortgage and could sell the house or take a career break or even give up working for a while, yet for the past few years, she'd been incapable of any kind of change.

Before the pandemic, she never imagined for one moment that she'd miss the days spent working nine to five in the City Hall. The Home Improvements Grants Department consisted of Bernice, Sheila and Siobhan, and they shared the open-plan office on the third floor with the Accounts Section, a larger team with about a dozen staff. Every day, the same old ding-dong in Bernice's section, Sheila and Siobhan chittering and caffling and complaining about their families, gossiping about everyone else behind their backs, making constant trips to the small kitchen shared by everyone on Floor 3, bemoaning the irony of working in Home Improvements but never doing any home renovations themselves, and generally wasting as much time as possible. Bernice did not like to think that she shared any traits with Sheila and Siobhan but sometimes she had to admit that maybe she was stuck in even more of a rut than they were.

When the new guy arrived in Accounts, Sheila and Siobhan mocked him mercilessly behind his back. A chunky young man with brown velvety eyes like a cow's, he hummed to himself in the elevator and on the stairs and he hummed as he strolled past the Home Improvement Grants Section on his way to the staff room bang on 1 p.m. every day, with a Tupperware container in his hand. When Sheila first heard the humming, she raised her eyebrows and whispered 'What kind of weirdo is that young lad?' Siobhan ambled out to the kitchen and reported back. 'A real Mammy's boy, heating up his dinner,' she said. 'It smells delicious though. Mammy sure can cook.'

The shared staff room on Floor 3 was small, with barely enough room for a water cooler, a kettle, a sink and the said microwave plus a table and six chairs. One lunchtime, soon after Ambrose had arrived at City Hall, Bernice was eating a perfectly decent cheese and salad sandwich when he hummed in and placed his container in the microwave. The aroma of his reheated meal was heavenly and when he took it out, she couldn't resist asking what it was.

'Just some leftover coq au vin with a bit of rice,' he said, looking down at his plate.

'Smells delicious,' said Bernice.

'Thanks,' he said. He smiled shyly at her then. 'Would you like some?'

'Oh no thanks, I'm fine.'

He sat his bulk carefully down on the chair opposite her and began to eat. 'I might have put in too many shallots.'

'You made it yourself?'

'Yeah. I love cooking.'

He ate with delicacy, she noted, as she took a bite of her now distinctly unappealing sandwich.

'I can hardly boil an egg myself.'

'My mother taught me. She was a brilliant cook.'

Bernice thought about her own mother. Mrs. Callinan had not been a domestic goddess, though she had made sure the family was well-dressed and never over-fed. A memory came, unwelcome. Her mother snarling across the kitchen table at her father. *Eat with your mouth shut.* Her brother raising his eyes to heaven. Herself, saying nothing, listening to the scraping sounds of knives and forks on the blue and white willow pattern plates. All dead now. She missed her humble father most and had been heartbroken by his demise. The deaths of her mother and her errant brother had been different. Even now, a sick mix of guilt and horror made her stomach turn whenever she recalled how they had died.

'My mother was hopeless,' said Bernice. 'Cooking made her cross.'

As the weeks went by, Bernice often found herself in the staff room at the same time as Ambrose. He talked a lot about food, but he was a sympathetic listener too.

'I'm saving up for a new kitchen,' Ambrose said one lunchtime, as he spooned half of his mushroom risotto into a bowl for her to eat. 'It's my dream. A gas hob with six burners, a really good electric oven, as much worktop space as possible for breadmaking and so on, loads of storage space for my bits and pieces.'

The kitchen back in Liberty Terrace was awful, Bernice knew. All dark brown cupboards and battered white appliances. She had realised, during therapy, that she needed either to make the house her own, or move. After the funerals, she'd bagged up the possessions of her mother and her brother and given them to a charity shop, but couldn't bring herself to do anything else, until a fitful effort a few months ago, when she'd painted her bedroom, bought a new king-size bed, took down the ancient floral curtains and replaced them with a set of wooden blinds.

'I'm planning a new kitchen myself,' she found herself saying.

'Really? Have you done much research?'

Bernice hadn't anticipated such a surge of interest from Ambrose. Soon, she was swept along by his enthusiasm — and the kitchen design magazines that he brought in, and the links to websites that he forwarded to her at an almost alarming rate.

Sheila and Siobhan took an interest too. It was a nice change from the disabled bathrooms, wheelchair ramps and wider doorways that they were used to dealing with in the Home Improvement Grants Section, and fortunately they knew who all the best builders were.

Lunchtimes on the third floor of City Hall became planning meetings for Bernice's kitchen. Ambrose began to spend his Saturdays ambling around the shops with her, helping her to choose the new appliances, the tiles, the fitted cupboards, even the kitchen sink.

During January and February, the workmen were in the house. The dust, the dirt, the delays, the dizzying confusion of it all. The makeshift arrangement with the microwave and kettle in the back bedroom. If Bernice had known what a palaver the whole thing would be, she might never have gone through with it. But at last, in early March, the work was done.

Ambrose had his back to her and was watching his food spin round in the microwave. 'How's the new kitchen?' he asked. 'I can hardly wait to see it.'

'It's perfect,' Bernice said. She hesitated. 'It's so perfect I'm intimidated by it. I haven't figured out how to use the oven yet.'

'Let me cook you dinner,' Ambrose said. 'I'll pretend I'm on *MasterChef*.'

The microwave dinged and Ambrose opened it. A delicious aroma of some kind of curry floated out. He'd been such a help to her. How could Bernice refuse? 'So long as you don't mention it to Sheila and Siobhan,' she said. 'We wouldn't want them to get the wrong idea.'

Ambrose agreed.

That Saturday evening, Ambrose arrived at Bernice's house with shopping bags of food and drink, his Kitchen Aid, a set of Sabatier knives and his Tefal deep fat fryer. He put a blue and white striped apron over his ample frame, slung a teacloth over his shoulder and set to work.

Bernice sat at her new kitchen counter, on one of her too-high brand new bar stools and sipped a glass of wine. She watched Ambrose as he hummed and chopped and sliced and diced and peeled and mixed and rolled and sieved and fried and basted and seared. Finally, Ambrose lowered crab beignets into the deep fat fryer, and the sizzling sound drowned out his humming and then he hummed again as he plated the first course delicately on two of her best plates, with a curve of home-made chilli mayonnaise and a slice of lemon.

When Bernice tasted Ambrose's starter, she felt all at once as if she was having a day at the seaside and a late-night visit to a fish and chip van. By the time she had eaten the main course of lapsang souchon-infused saddle of venison with root vegetables and smoked pancetta sauce she was slightly tipsy — and they hadn't even started on dessert.

Then one thing led to another and they ended up in bed.

Oh, the breakfast next day... perfect hangover food. A Bloody Mary to take the edge off. That man could really poach an egg. He made a hollandaise sauce to die for. His rashers were done to perfection and his mushrooms, cooked in the bacon fat with crushed garlic and chopped parsley were simply divine.

As Bernice drove out the Straight Road toward Ballincollig, she remembered that Ambrose lived somewhere in the hinterland. She had never been to his place. She wondered how he was coping with the Lockdown. At least he surely kept a well-stocked larder. She wondered what it would be like when they were all back at work again; whether he'd pretend those two weekends never happened or simply ignore her.

He had rung her a few hours after the Government announced the Lockdown.

'The way things are going, I'm not going see you for ages,' he had said. 'We'll all be working from home. And I'm outside the two-kilometre limit.'

'That's a shame,' she said.

'I think maybe... should I move in with you?'

She had been taken aback. 'You must be kidding.'

'No, I'm not.' Ambrose sounded aggrieved.

'But...'

'I know what you're going to say. It's far too soon. But I think we should see where this relationship goes.'

Relationship? It was just two weekends. He was far too young for her. He was a work colleague. It was never going to last anyway. Nothing ever did.

'You could move in with me instead,' he said. 'Only you have a much nicer kitchen.'

'So, it's only my kitchen you're interested in?' she said. She knew she sounded ratty.

'Well if that's what you think,' he said. 'Fine.' He had driven over to her house in high dudgeon and collected his Kitchen Aid and his pasta maker. After he'd left, she realised he'd forgotten his deep fat fryer. She had texted him but he had not texted her in return. So immature of him. It just proved that she was right. The whole thing would have been a disaster.

Bernice parked in the ground floor car park underneath the supermarket. She put on her face mask, sanitized her hands, grabbed a sanitized trolley and stood on a yellow arrow sign behind a line of lonely shoppers who waited for a Stop and Go sign to turn green, while other lonesome shoppers emerged, their trolleys and wire baskets filled with what they'd foraged. Within a few minutes Bernice had pushed her empty trolley inside and onto the travellator and, as she ascended to the first floor, it clung steadfastly to the magnetised surface while she clung grimly to its handle. When she reached the top and trundled forward onto solid ground, the supermarket seemed eerily quiet, with only murmured conversations at the cash tills, the incessant geeky beep of products being passed over scanners, the shuffling of packages, the clink of wire baskets and an automated voice saying *Thank you for shopping at Tesco.* Bernice stood for a moment in confusion as the shopping aisles stretched out ahead of her. No children bickered with parents over which kind of biscuits to buy, no couples lingered at the deli counter. Everyone seemed to be alone, like her, as the smells of baked goods and antibacterial cleaner mingled in the air. She took her shopping list out of her pocket and tried to focus.

Potatoes, carrots, onions, garlic... she noticed that underneath her mask her breath was kind of stinky. She wondered if she'd always had bad breath or if wearing the mask made it so, and, as she pondered this, she wondered if the brown mushrooms would last longer than the paler ones and if she should bother buying fruit, when most of it would go off before she got round to eating it. Then, she heard the humming.

She'd heard that sound before. Ambrose hummed like that. He always hummed that way. She'd know it anywhere. She'd heard it so often, ever since the first time he had hummed past the Home Improvement Grants Section on Floor 3 of the City Hall. Surely it couldn't be Ambrose? She felt her heart sink into her stomach and leap back up again. The humming sound grew more distant, so she began to push her trolley towards the direction it had emanated from. The frozen food aisle. His mask was one of those blue disposable ones and he wore the navy padded jacket he always wore, but he was thinner, she thought. There he was, putting a packet of frozen spinach into his trolley and it put her in mind of the time Ambrose cooked salmon on a bed of spinach with a white wine and tarragon sauce and Hasselbach potatoes. She felt desperately sad. He had stroked her hair in bed. No one else had ever called her delicious.

From a distance Bernice stared, as the man who looked like Ambrose, oblivious of her presence, pushed his trolley towards the dairy section. She deserted her own trolley and tiptoed around the corner to watch him contemplating cheeses. While he had his back to her, she considered the contents of his trolley. The melon struck Bernice as odd, and there were far too many courgettes in there for one person, plus a hell of a lot of cleaning products. Two dozen eggs but no sausages or rashers or Clonakilty pudding.

No wine in his trolley. No gin. No lager. The Ambrose who had come to her house on those two glorious food-filled weekends in March had carefully chosen a different wine for every course, and a suitable lager to accompany his spicier dishes. Maybe he'd stocked up in Winsome Wines. Maybe he'd given up alcohol during Lockdown. Maybe he'd changed. Maybe it wasn't him but a — what was it called again — a doppelgänger? He seemed too thin but still, the ungainly walk, the humming, that anorak. How could he be thinner when everyone else was putting on Covid weight? Come to think of it, maybe Ambrose had a new healthy lifestyle. He was probably seeing someone else. Someone he went walking with. Jogging, even. An attractive person who appreciated him and never had to go to therapy and had nice hair even when the hair salons were closed.

But he was about to turn back and she feared that he might see her, so she darted into the tinned goods aisle, where she felt she was in safer territory. She had upset Ambrose. She had hurt his feelings. He would not want anything more to do with her. She walked up the aisle and turned around at the top, searching for her deserted trolley. Back in the tinned goods section, she pulled herself together and clunked a four-pack of tinned tomatoes into her trolley, followed by tins of tuna and a multi-pack of baked beans. Tins, she thought, were safe. Tins would last ages. She threw a giant pack of fusilli on top of her tins.

As she pushed her trolley onwards, to where she thought Household Products might be, she told herself not to be so pathetic, to stop being such a loser, that she was doing fine on her own. But she hankered after Ambrose now, missed the way he hummed as he chopped and sliced and diced and peeled and mixed and rolled and sieved and fried and basted and seared. She missed his sea trout with potato puree, pea puree and spinach with nutmeg. She missed his mushroom risotto. She missed his chicken cacciatore. She missed his paella. She missed the way he had stroked her hair in bed, as if she was a little cat. She missed the way he had tried, and failed, to put his socks on while standing up. The sex. She missed the sex. All I want, she realised, is for Ambrose to make me a meal — and make a meal of me.

Oh my God, I've lost him, she thought. Where is he? She picked up her pace and peered around corners and down aisles, stopping now and then to listen for his humming.

She should at least apologise. What should she say? Something casual. Not too needy. How about *Oh, it's you Ambrose. I nearly didn't recognise you with your mask on.* No, that was completely inappropriate. Jesus, that sounded like 'I hardly recognised you with your clothes on'. Cop on to yourself Bernice. She'd just say a friendly hello, and wait for his reaction. Maybe he was still hurt or maybe he wouldn't be interested in her any more or maybe he'd act as if nothing had ever happened between them at all.

But where was he? Maybe he'd already paid and left. She'd have to be logical. No time to meander, hoping to hear the humming again. She began to speed up, racing her trolley up and down each product aisle, looking frantically around her as she went, narrowly avoiding contact with other shoppers, with other shopping trolleys. Up and down she went, steering wildly, her face sodden from sweat underneath her mask.

She rolled her trolley past the tills, checking each and every queue. No Ambrose. But there he was, his trolley brimming over with chock-full plastic bags, way ahead beyond the cash tills, ambling towards the exit.

As she watched, he reached the travellator and pushed his trolley ahead of him. She could see his head disappearing as he descended. Down, down, down. He'd be in the car park in a few seconds.

'Ambrose!' she called out. 'Ambrose, I've still got your deep fat fryer.'

Her voice rang out loud above the clinking beeping shuffling mumbling trundling wheeling sounds. She shoved her half-full trolley aside and began to run.

HOME IMPROVEMENTS

It was a Friday afternoon in late October. Henry's final Zoom meeting was over. The kids were home from school. He could hear them upstairs playing Fortnite on the computer with the sound turned up full blast. Since the first Lockdown in March he'd been working from home. His office was in the front room. Marcia worked at the kitchen table but she only worked part-time anyway; Monday, Tuesday and Wednesday, doing accounts for Downeys, the building firm. In March, Marcia had set up his old laptop and a new computer in the children's bedrooms. He had said it wasn't healthy but she had said what choice do we have — they both needed to be online while the schools were closed. The house was too small. He had to get out before he exploded.

He plodded into the kitchen. 'I've got to go to the office.'

The loaf of bread she'd used for lunchtime sandwiches was still on the kitchen table, the crusts of bread, crumbs of cheese on plates, the children's half-drunk glasses of milk, the tub of coleslaw, their coffee mugs, a half-eaten goldgrain biscuit. Marcia hadn't even bothered putting the milk back in the fridge. She stood there, paintbrush in hand. On the kitchen counter next to the kettle was a selection of small tins of paint. Testers, he thought they were called. On the cream-coloured wall to the right of the back door were several swathes of colour: light blue, yellow, dark green, a greeny-blue that might be turquoise, a light purple and, worst of all, a pinkish red. She's going slowly nuts, he thought. The colours seemed ridiculous to him.

Marcia pointed to the dark green, her eyebrows raised.

'No?' she asked.

'No,' said Henry, shaking his head.

She picked up a brush and painted a streak of lilac next to the purple. 'No,' she said quietly, almost to herself.

'No?' he asked. The lilac didn't seem too bad to him. Well, it wasn't great but it was the best of a bad lot.

'No.' She sighed and walked past him, still holding the paintbrush. She went to the sink and turned on the tap. As she rinsed the paintbrush under the cold water he went over to the kettle and lifted it up, to gauge whether there was enough water in it for a cup of tea.

He held the kettle, waiting for her to finish rinsing the brush so he could fill it. It seemed to take forever. She hummed while she held the brush under the running water, riffling her fingers through the bristles as if she were washing a child's hair. Her face was pale and taut, she hardly ever wore make-up these days. She was wearing her old grey sweatpants and an oversized black top, but even so, he could see that her body had become more toned in the past few months. She'd become addicted to some YouTube exercise thing—every morning before she woke the kids, there she was on the mat in front of the TV, doing stretches and bends, lifting tins of baked beans up and down, balancing on a round plastic ball she'd bought online. In the evenings, before she cooked the dinner, she went out jogging. Not that he'd benefitted much from her efforts. She always seemed tired in bed.

'I can't decide,' she said, flicking the bristles of the paintbrush underneath the tap.

He was still holding the kettle. He put it down.

Oh, fuck it. A beer, he thought. That's what he needed. A cold beer after a hard day's work. He put the kettle down and opened the fridge. The six-pack he'd bought yesterday gleamed at him in welcome. He fumbled a can out of its plastic harness. It felt cold to the touch. He pushed the fridge door closed. Then he snapped the tab of the lager can open.

Marcia turned around.

'No,' she said crossly.

'No?' he said. 'No?'

'Jesus Christ, Henry, it's only four o'clock. You'll be sat in front of the TV by five, snoring like a hyena. And then pacing the house all night.'

'It's Friday.' He drank directly from the can. It tasted fizzy and metallic. Not like going to the pub after work. Nothing like a proper pint. He wished he was in the Long Valley right now. That Friday feeling, skiving off early with the gang from work, torn packets of Taytos and KP peanuts splayed on the marble top of the big round table near the back wall of the pub, a pint of Heineken in a cold damp glass, cracking jokes with the lads, flirting outrageously with Alison as she sipped from her usual glass of Sauvignon, their affair hidden in plain sight.

'At the very least, pour it into a glass. There could be rat pee on those cans.' She plonked the paintbrush down on the draining board, took a glass out of a top cupboard and handed it to him. He poured the rest of the lager into the glass and threw the can into one of the bins.

'That goes in the recyling,' she said.

He put the glass down. He took the can out of one bin and put it in another.

'I'd like to get it done this weekend but I can't decide what colour. I'm tending toward the cerise.'

'Cerise?'

'Yeah, the pinkish colour.'

'You're not serious.'

'I'm not sure yet but I kind of like it.'

'I have to go to the office,' he said.

'Now? I thought you were finished for the day.'

'Some files I have to pick up, for Monday.'

'Can you pick up a chicken? I'd need to put it in the oven by five at the latest though.'

He made for the door.

'Don't forget to take off your slippers.'

Sure enough, he had almost left the house without noticing he still had his slippers on. Upstairs he took a shoebox from the bottom of the wardrobe. Inside was a pair of stone-coloured suede shoes. He took a second to admire them as he tied the shoelaces. They were exactly like his old blue ones. 'Casual but smart,' he thought. He'd ordered them online and miraculously they'd arrived within two weeks and were exactly what he'd wanted.

Outside, the black woman from Number 3 and her little girl were in the park across the street, throwing a frisbee back and forth. They were splashes of colour in the dull afternoon, the little girl in bright yellow, the mother in flowery pink, the purple frisbee. The mother had a big arse and heavy breasts but a nice shape to her all the same. He wondered what she'd look like naked, and whether she shaved her pubic hair. It would be dark and springy. Marcia hadn't got herself waxed since the younger one was born, five years ago. She rarely even shaved, except her legs and armpits. I've had enough of suffering, she said. Plus, she wasn't going to risk another ingrown hair.

Marcia was more interested in interior decorating now. Before she started working for the Downeys she had been reluctant to do anything to the house unless it made the place more saleable. They'd clamber up the housing ladder soon. They'd sell the house and buy a bigger one, then a bigger one, and eventually, when the kids were older, maybe buy a site and build a house of their own design. (He was an architectural technician, though he often called himself an architect, in company.) Now she simply worked away, one small home improvement at a time, and didn't bother to consult him.

He had no reason to go to the office on the other side of the city. He wasn't supposed to go there at all. Only the directors did. He wasn't a director. That spot of bother a couple of years ago with the intern had put the tin hat on that. Young women these days were so touchy. They simply couldn't take a joke. Thank God for girls like Alison.

He drove into town and parked in Tesco Car Park. He went to the English Market. Near the eternally dry fountain, O'Sullivan's Poultry featured the usual array of chickens, duck, those BBQ and spicy chicken wings and legs that the two kids were mad for, kebabs, quails' eggs. He stood on a yellow line until it was his turn. The young blonde woman was serving. She wore a white apron, a white face mask and heaps of eye makeup. He knew better than to indulge in small talk; she was another one with zero sense of humour. He asked for an average-sized stuffed chicken and she rang it up, put it in a white plastic bag and handed it to him across the glass counter.

The Chocolate Shop was only two steps away. He considered buying a small box of chocolates but settled for a box of rose-flavoured Turkish Delight. He had always had a liking for Hadji Bey, ever since he was a child. He fired it into the plastic bag and made his way through the market, past Heaven's Cakes, O'Flynn's Gourmet Sausages, the Olive Stall, the Alternative Bread Company. He passed the Roughty Fruit King, which no longer sold fruit but artisan chocolate, honey, fancy biscuits. Meat, more meat, that rank smell of raw meat. He only liked it when it was cooked. Superfruit on the right and then he was outside on Grand Parade and could take off his mask and breathe properly again.

On Nano Nagle Bridge, a beggar sat in the weak autumn sun, a cardboard box on the ground in front of him. At least it wasn't raining. Outside the Quay Co-op he stopped to text her.

> Finished work. Need to drop something off
> to you. Will be there in a few minutes.

Alison's place was a fancy new residential development on White Street called Maison Verre. Developers were always wanting stupid names but maybe the architects had come up with this one. It wasn't all glass as the name suggested; it looked as if it was made of giant red and white Lego. 21st Century Irish Modernism was what they called it in the office. He looked around before dodging into the courtyard in case anyone who knew him happened to be about. Cork was such a small city you'd need to be doggy wide if you didn't want people to know all your business. He put his mask on before he pressed the bell.

'Hello gorgeous,' he said as soon as she opened the door of her apartment.

'You shouldn't be here, really.'

She didn't seem all that pleased to see him, but then again, the pandemic was turning everyone into nervous wrecks. He tried to kiss her in the hallway but she shrugged him off and led him into her kitchen.

On her marble-topped kitchen table, an exotic-looking array of flowers stood in a heavy vase. A bulbous pale green cactus-looking thing, sharp green fronds, red and purple angular blooms that looked like birds, something that looked like a head of cabbage, a few roses here and there, some flowers that looked like giant coloured daisies. He put the plastic bag on the table next to them. He took out the box of Turkish Delight and presented it to her. She scarcely even looked at it.

'You shouldn't be here,' she said.

'Ah come on. I won't stay long.'

'Well, at least go and wash your hands.'

He went to her downstairs bathroom, had a piss and washed his hands. There was another flower arrangement on the top of the bathroom cabinet, fronds of dried reeds and rushes that seemed fake, yet once he touched them he could tell that they had once grown from the earth.

Afterwards, they lay in Alison's bed. The room was white, the bed was huge and modern, with a pale grey headboard and matching bedlinen in white and grey. Through the window, a triangle of crisp autumn sun fell across the end of the bed.

She'd been reluctant at first but in the end he'd given her a good seeing to, just like old times. He felt fine now. Absolutely fine. He stretched his arms out, above his head, and considered the width of the bed. He wondered, briefly, if a bigger bed and a bigger house would have made a difference to his marriage. 'What do you call this size of bed again?'

'It's a Super King,' she said. 'When my ex-husband and I first met, he had an awful bed that sagged in the middle like a hammock with old springs that made terrible pronging noises. I had a smelly old futon that wasn't much better. I always wanted a decent bed but it was years before we could afford one.'

'How wide is it?'

'Six feet.'

'Everyone should have a bed this size.'

'One time, soon after we bought it, I was asleep, completely covered up in the duvet, head and all... my ex got up first and went downstairs and he couldn't find me anywhere. Eventually, he got so worried he went back to the bedroom, intending to get dressed so he could go out and look for me. I was inside in bed under the covers the whole time, fast asleep.' She smiled at the memory and then her face changed. 'We were so in love,' she said. 'I messed the whole thing up.'

She rolled away from him and sat up against the headboard. 'This was a mistake. I can't believe I let it happen. You're just so great at canoodling and getting your own way but...'

'Ah Alison. I'm not a Covid risk. I hardly see anyone.'

'No. That's not the point. Even if it was, your kids are back in school now. My mother is cocooning and I have to do her shopping so I need to be dead careful. And how about your wife?'

'She sees nobody. It's fine.'

'No, Henry. No, it's not fine.' She got out of bed and slipped on a rose-coloured dressing gown. 'It's over.'

'You're joking,' he said merrily.

'No. It's not just about Covid. I'm seeing someone,' she said, with her back turned to him. 'A guy called Donal. It's monogamy all the way for me from now on. This was just a farewell fuck.' She turned around to look at him. 'Off you go now,' she said, the way one would speak to a child, and left the room.

He lay there for a moment, wondering if it was a joke. Then he gathered up his clothes and dressed.

The street outside was dark now, and a cold breeze blew across the river as he made his way down the quayside. Well, to hell with her anyway, herself and her big bed and her minimalist décor, he thought. In all of his liaisons, he had had the decency to end them on a proper note, not like her, with her insolence. Off you go now, she'd said, as if she couldn't care less. He, at least, on these occasions, had always had the decency to feign regret. The sound of an ambulance in the distance made him shiver. His new shoes felt too tight as he crossed the bridge and walked slowly back to the car park. In the car, his hand shook as he tried to insert his key in the ignition.

In the hallway, Henry heard the sound of the computer upstairs. Shockingly, he felt as if he might burst into tears at any moment. His late father, accountant, sacristan and dictator, used to say that children should be seen but not heard. Henry had never wanted to behave like him. He had heard his kids today, but he had not seen them. He longed to see them now. He went upstairs and into Mark's room. Mark was sitting at the blinking computer, furiously gunning down enemies. Little

Annie was propped up on Mark's bed, poking at her iPad.

'Hey guys,' said Henry, folding his arms casually as he leaned against the door jamb. 'How was your day?'

Annie glanced up once and muttered 'Fine' before returning her gaze to the iPad. Mark didn't seem to hear him at all.

In the kitchen, Marcia was leaning back in a kitchen chair, her feet stretched out on another, as she held her smartphone to her ear. The oven was on and he could smell something cooking. He realised that he was starving.

'Ah, that's brilliant, thanks.' She was talking into the phone and smiling at the far wall. 'I really appreciate it.'

On the table, a bottle stood in a wine bucket he hadn't seen before, next to her half-empty glass. Next to it, a vase held a complicated bouquet of flowers.

He reached into a cupboard for a glass, poured himself some wine and sat down. God, he needed it. He felt dizzy.

'Thanks a million,' she said. 'Yeah, you too. Bye bye bye bye bye.' She put her phone down on the table, then looked at him as if she hadn't noticed him come in.

'Where did those come from?' The flowers looked familiar. The same, yet different, to the ones in Alison's kitchen.

'Oh, Donal had them delivered. A thank you for all my hard work.'

'Donal?'

'Donal Downey, one of my bosses. He says once construction is back in full swing, he's going to offer me a full-time permanent position.'

'That's good.' He drained his glass.

'You took your time. Where's the chicken?'

He could see the white plastic bag containing the dead

bird now, in his mind's eye. He'd left it there, on that other kitchen table, next to another vase of strange exotic flowers.

'I partly guessed you'd forget. It doesn't matter. I made a macaroni cheese with spinach and bacon — it's in the oven. Just as well I had a back-up plan.' She leaned over to refill her wine glass, then took another sip.

'By the way, I've decided.' She waved her hand towards the back door. 'I'm going with the cerise.'

The wall next to the back door now bore a large rough-edged square of deep pink.

'Donal's so decent. He's getting one of his lads to collect the paint and drop it here in the morning for me.'

She was wearing makeup, he noticed. Her lips were almost the same colour as the paint on the wall.

THE GREAT LOCKDOWN RESCUE

It's a gilt-framed mirror on a wooden stand, the kind you can turn around so your face is normal on one side and magnified to a horrendous degree on the other. It belonged to Glenda; her vanity mirror she called it. She used to sit at the dressing table upstairs and peer into it while she put her makeup on. I brought the mirror downstairs this morning and put it on the kitchen table, thinking I might as well cut my hair myself, to distract myself from everything, but now I'm not so sure about it.

At least I've a fine head of hair, I tell myself as I look at my reflection. It's completely white now, but it's still as thick as a good-sized paintbrush. I'm not a vain man by any stretch of the imagination but I've always been pleased enough that I'm not bald like a lot of other men of my vintage. Glenda, God rest her soul, always loved my hair, but it's so long now that I look like a demented old hippie. I should have gone to Short Cuts in August when I had the chance. My eyes are bloodshot too. I look like shit. I feel like shit. I know Martin has a few cans of lager in the fridge. All I really want to do today is to drink myself into oblivion. But I can't do that. I went mad on the drink after Glenda died and I know only too well that it's not a road I should go down again.

I sit down at the kitchen table in front of the mirror and turn it so it's the normal side. I tilt it so I can see my reflection and adjust the kitchen towel around my shoulders. Then I take the kitchen scissors in one hand and a clump of my hair in the other. My hand is shaking so I put the scissors down again. It seemed like a good way to pass the time, but now I fear I'll make a pure hames of it.

For the umpteenth time, I look over at the empty dog bed in the corner of the kitchen. It's a big rectangular cushion covered in some kind of brown plush material with an off-white paw print pattern. Spike's favourite ball on a rope and his much-chewed rubber chicken are thrown in on top of it. The young eejit, Martin, loves buying toys for the dog. There's a rake of them in the cupboard under the stairs. He even bought a black studded collar, punk style for the dog but I said no way, it didn't suit him. Spike is the friendliest dog you could ever meet and handsome too. He's a medium-sized German Schnauzer with soft grey fur and a white muzzle, a little beard and a thoughtful look on his face. Myself and Glenda had a dog one time — Rusty, a little terrier — but when he died she said she couldn't bear to go through that again. So we didn't get another.

Martin turned up four years ago, a year after Glenda died. He was like a stray dog himself, with nowhere to live and somehow I ended up letting him stay, though he isn't even my own flesh and blood and I'm old enough to be his grandad. I got used to having Martin around. He's an orphan with only a mad oul stepfather out in Ballincollig and he's a simple enough lad, mad about dogs. He said if we got one he'd walk it and do all the chores so I gave in. Spike cost a fair whack of money but he was worth every cent. As soon as I laid eyes on him I knew he was the dog for us. Now he's gone.

Two days ago, young Martin brought the dog out for a walk as usual. He came back in an awful state. He'd tied Spike onto a lamp post outside Lennox's and went in to get a bag of chips and by the time he came out, the dog was nowhere to be seen. After all I've done for the little blaggard. The careless little bollix. I went ballistic.

Well, we headed off to Anglesea Garda station straight away to report it.

'I tied him up carefully. He didn't just get loose,' said Martin. 'A small girl waiting in the queue with her mother saw the fella that took him away. A black denim jacket, she said, and a snake tattoo on his neck.'

The Ban Garda at the front desk was a nice enough girl but she didn't seem to think there was much hope. The police are up to ninety during the pandemic what with patrolling the empty streets and standing at road blocks trying to stop people from travelling beyond the 5 km but what I wanted was action and all she did was tell us to use social media and put up posters. 'Dog theft has escalated since the pandemic began,' she said. 'So many people want pets because they're home all the time. There's a lot of money to be made, especially with pedigree dogs like your one. Still, we'll do our best for you. At least he's microchipped.'

Well, my head hasn't been the best, the past few months, stuck inside, cocooning, going off my rocker with boredom, hearing about people sick and dying. The first Lockdown was alright, like a second Christmas holiday with lots of food and television. The second Lockdown is stranger. Martin's been binge-watching every single *Star Trek* season from start to finish on that Netflix and it's annoying. I only like the first series, with Captain Kirk. Glenda and myself used to sit on the couch and watch crime dramas, like *Kojak* and *Colombo*. She'd put her little feet in my lap. Lefty and Righty, I called her feet. The feet would talk in high little voices, commenting on the action. A silly little joke. William and Glenda and Lefty and Righty. Maybe it was because we had no children. Only Glenda's feet. When Glenda died she was only sixty-nine. What I really want is to go to the pub and get plastered. But the pubs are closed. I think I should allow myself one of those cans from the fridge.

The past two nights, since Spike got stolen, I haven't been able to sleep. I've been demented imagining all kinds of awful situations, the poor dog wondering what the hell is going on. He could be anywhere. Martin says some of these dognappers take the dogs to England on the ferry and make a fortune out of them. He's been on the internet non-stop or else he's out walking the streets searching for Spike and putting up 'Lost Dog' posters with a photo of Spike and an offer of a reward and his mobile number. His phone keeps pinging with messages but they are all rubbish or sympathy and there's not a sign of Spike. At night Martin's been pacing around the house til all hours, foostering and fidgeting on the computer in his bedroom, cursing to himself and whimpering. Serves him right. I've lost all patience with the lad.

This morning, I gave him a right dressing-down. He

hasn't an ounce of sense. He forgot to lock the back door last night. Anyone could hop over the wall and get in. We could have been murdered in our beds. And the eejit made himself an oven pizza in the middle of the night and only ate half of it. Wilful waste makes woeful want, I told him, not for the first time.

'I know. I'm fucking useless. No need to rub it in.' Martin went off out the door then, with another sheaf of posters and I haven't seen him since. I could really do with a drink. Those cans of lager — there's four of them in the fridge.

I look at my thirsty, sad old face in the mirror. Glenda would sit in front of it, upstairs, for ages, dabbing all kinds of stuff on her face, before she put her glad rags on. She loved getting all dolled up to go out. Even when she got sick, she still made an effort, put the bit of lipstick on, sprayed herself with that Cacharel perfume I used to buy her every Christmas.

I didn't marry Glenda with false intentions. I loved her dearly and when I found out that I'd short-changed her — that I couldn't give her children — I went on the drink big time. In the end, she told me I had to stop drinking or she'd leave me. 'Sure we have each other,' she said. I quit the drink then. We never said another word about it. Five years ago, she left me anyway, for good. After the funeral I went back on the booze again.

Deckie Google came in to Cissie Young's one afternoon, dragged me out of the pub, shoved me in his car and drove me to my doctor's surgery and then put me in the car again and drove me to Cuan Mhuire to dry out. The counsellor in the clinic told me I was obviously finding it difficult to cope on my own. No shit, Sherlock, I nearly said to her.

A bluebottle is buzzing at the kitchen window. The panes of glass are filthy and badly need cleaning. Myself and Martin have been stuck in the house for months yet neither of us seem to find the time to clean the damn place. Glenda would be appalled. She was always very clean. Cobwebs in the corners, at least the spiders are working hard. Jesus, I'm dying for a drink.

I get up to open the window and shoo the dirty bluebottle out. It's the self-same window Martin broke four years ago or more, when he broke in. He thought the place was empty, that I was dead. He'd mixed me up with that oddball, Albert Clarke in Number One, who went into a coma. I didn't have the heart to kick the lad out. He was so young, so gormless. He couldn't even find a proper squat. Glenda used to say that I didn't suffer fools gladly. Sometimes she said it like it was a bad thing. I can be harsh at times. I know I'm not as kind as she was. I let the young lad stay, partly because I figured his presence would keep me off the booze. Yes, I've always been a small bit selfish. But I felt sorry for him too.

'Fuck this for a game of soldiers,' I say out loud. I take a can of lager out of the fridge. It feels nice and cold. I can handle one. I'll drink it slow. To hell with everything. If I can't have a drink now... I know I shouldn't but... I'm just about to pop the tab when I hear the front door opening and I know it's Martin and he knows I never drink and he'll drive me mad asking questions so I shove the can of lager quickly back in the fridge before he bursts into the kitchen.

'I found the fella that stole Spike. I know where he lives.' He looks around the kitchen frantically. 'Where's my charger?' He spots it on the kitchen counter and plugs his phone in. 'I could hear dogs barking in his back yard only the wall is fierce high and I couldn't see over it and I took a couple of photos so I'd remember the place and I was going to ring the cops only my phone went out of charge.'

'What? You found the langer?'

'Yeah. He was following a woman with a small dog, some kind of poodle and he totally fit the description the little girl at the chipper gave me — a snake tattoo on his neck, so...' Martin is up to high doh, talking so fast I can hardly understand what he's saying. 'So I tailed him, like in the crime books. We got to do something. If we don't act fast the dogs might be gone.'

My heart is hopping up and down in my chest as if it's on an elastic band. I hope I'm not going to have a heart attack. 'Deckie Google used to be high up in the police. Maybe he can pull some strings.'

I put my shoes on and grab my jacket and go outside. Martin follows. I knock on Deckie Google's door and wait.

Jake O'Sullivan from No. 7 is standing across the road, waving his arms like windmills, then stretching them up to the sky and down again. He's wearing a shirt and a tie that has come askew, with a pair of grey tracksuit bottoms and trainers. He crosses the street and begins to talk at us from two metres away as if he's been locked up for days. 'I've had three Team meetings today and one Zoom. My eyes are going to fall out of my head, if I don't tear them out first. And the baby doesn't sleep. I don't know what we're doing wrong. It wasn't like this with our first.'

'We've got an emergency,' I tell him. 'Martin's found the

fella who stole our dog.'

Just then, Deckie opens his front door and peers out. As usual he's perfectly turned out, in a neat jacket, a matching navy facemask and polished leather shoes.

'Deckie, we've located the dog thief. Tell him, Martin.'

Martin blathers the whole story out again to Deckie.

Jake stands there listening, as he squeezes his eyes tight shut and opens them again a couple of times.

Deckie frowns. 'I'll ring it in to the station,' he says, as if he was still a Chief Inspector in the Garda, even though he's been retired for years. He takes out his mobile phone and rings Anglesea Street Police Station and in seconds he's onto someone he obviously knows. He talks for a few moments about a stolen dog and his urgent need for a squad car and a search warrant, then he holds the phone to his chest for a moment and turns to Martin. 'Do you have the address?' he asked.

'Not exactly,' Martin said. 'But I know where it is.'

Deckie puts the phone up to his mouth again. 'Ah sure I know ye're up to your eyeballs,' he says to the person on the other end. 'Sorry, I can't hear you, no, sorry, you're breaking up. I'll sort it out and phone you back.' He turns to me and says, 'Useless. Bloody useless. We'll get the dog ourselves. I'll go and get me car keys.'

This is worrying. I've noticed how long it takes Deckie to park. His eyesight isn't what it used to be. I don't drive any more myself. I gave up soon after poor Siofra O'Sullivan, God rest her soul, slammed her Audi TT into the back of my car. Jake, however, has a proper family car; a blue Audi Estate with a big boot and a child seat in the back. Deckie notices my hesitation.

'So long as we all wear our masks,' he says. 'It's only a short trip.'

'Maybe Jake could take us,' I say.

'Me?'

Martin chips in. 'Would you mind driving us, Jake? It's only a few minutes away.' He shows us photos on his phone. A street view that looks familiar. A front door. A wall that looks about six feet high.

'Oh God yeah. Right.' Jake stops blinking. 'Let's do it,' he says. In seconds he's gone home for his car keys. In another few seconds he's back, unlocking his car and beckoning us over.

'Hang on,' I say, remembering the photos Martin showed us. 'Let's think about this. Martin, will you go in and get that aluminium stepladder from under the stairs. And dog food, in case we need it.'

'I'll take out the child seats while you're gone,' says Jake. 'We might need the space.'

By the time Martin comes back with the folding steps and a pack of Pedigree Complete, the rest of us are sitting in Jake's car. Jake and Deckie are in front, and I'm in the back. Martin shoves the stepladder in the boot. It just about fits though the top is poking over the back headrest. Martin sits into the back next to me. He's wearing one of the cheap black facemasks from Dealz. I'm wearing another. Deckie, in the front passenger seat, is wearing his navy fabric mask. Jake switches on the ignition and turns around. 'So we're all set?' he says. He's wearing a black mask too. 'We look like a bunch of vigilantes,' he says. Martin leans into the front to give Jake directions.

Outside the dog-napper's house, Deckie takes out some kind of warrant card — it must be ancient — and knocks briskly on the front door. Nothing happens. He knocks again, while we peer through the windows. No one seems to be home.

'Right,' says Deckie. 'Round the back.'

I can hear dogs barking and yelping and I'm sure I recognise Spike's bark. I feel desperate to jump over that goddam wall but it's way too high.

'Put up the stepladder,' I say. Jake gets the stepladder out of the boot and sets it up against the wall. Martin holds it steady while I clamber up and look over the wall. Jesus, my heart nearly jumps out of my mouth. There are six wire cages in the yard. Spike, my lovely dog, is in one of them. 'He's here! Spike's here!' I tell the lads. 'Spike, good boy, good boy. Don't worry Spike, we've come to get you,' My voice sounds squeaky and high. 'There's six cages but only four dogs.'

'We'll have to take the lot of them,' said Deckie. 'No dog gets left behind.'

All the dogs were barking now.

'Take it easy there now, William,' says Deckie. 'Come down and we'll send Martin over.'

I really want to go over the wall and jump down and tear those cages open but I can see his point, so I reverse down the ladder. I feel shaky enough when I get back on solid ground.

'Thanks be to God,' I say. 'Thanks be to God.'

Jake holds the ladder while Martin climbs up and straddles the top of the wall. Jake pushes the stepladder up towards Martin who pulls it up with some difficulty and drops it down on the other side. Then he disappears. The dogs are all yipping and yelping on the other side of the wall. The streets are empty, except for a man out jogging who runs past but doesn't seem to take any interest in our doings.

'I'd say give them a bit of food there, to calm them down,' shouts Deckie.

Jake takes the bag of Pedigree Complete and hurls it

over the wall.

'Jesus, that nearly hit me on the head.' Martin's voice sounds high and nervous. 'Oh Spike, oh Spike,' he's saying now.

'How is he?' I shout.

'He's fine,' Martin shouts back. 'I've got him out of the cage. The cages aren't locked, only bolted.'

My eyes are wet. Jake shouts 'Nice one!' and then 'How will we get them out?'

'Spike would be a bit heavy to carry up the ladder and over the wall,' says Deckie.

'And imagine if we dropped him.' Jake looks anxious.

'Check out the back gate, Martin!'

We run round the back and the padlocked gate rattles as Martin shoves it back and forth. 'No key in the lock,' he says. 'Could we cut the chain?'

'I have a wrench in the car,' says Jake and he races off to get it.

'Hang on,' says Martin's disembodied voice. 'Maybe we could take them through the house.'

'Good idea,' I shout.

In a minute Martin's back. 'We're good to go! The dopey fucker forgot to lock his back door!'

We all make a dash round to the front of the house again and in a moment the front door opens and there's Spike, lolloping out, over the moon to see me, wheeling around in delighted circles, lepping up and down, licking me all over my face. 'Good boy,' I say. 'Good boy.' I have to turn my face into his fur so no one can see the state of me.

Martin goes back inside and emerges with a Cocker Spaniel. Jake takes hold of the dog and calms it down. Then Martin appears again with a Jack Russell and hands it to Deckie. Finally, he emerges holding a nervy Red Setter by his collar, and pulls the door closed behind him.

Jake is driving. The Cocker Spaniel is in front, crouched on Deckie's lap, head sticking out the window and his ears blowing back in the breeze. The nervy Red Setter sits on his haunches in the back seat, between Martin and myself. The Jack Russell stands on Martin's lap, head out the back window, tongue lolling. I cradle Spike on my lap. I can't stop talking to him, telling him how glad I am to see him. Telling him that we're bringing him home. Telling him that we'll never ever lose him again. I feel elated. We're on Hope Street now and we're almost home.

I look across at Martin, and I get a shock. Tears are trickling down his cheeks. The poor lad. He played a blinder. I don't know what to say. Maybe Glenda would know, but she's not here.

I want to say the right thing. What is there to say?

I reach over and pat him on the back. 'Good boy,' I say. 'Now, now. You're a good boy.'

ACKNOWLEDGEMENTS

Acknowledgements are due to the following publications in which versions of some of these stories first appeared: *Looking at the Stars — An Anthology of Irish Writing* (2016) featured 'To Be a Dearborne' (titled 'Census'); *Surge: New Writing From Ireland* (O'Brien Press, 2014) featured 'Quality Time'; *The Elysian: Creative Responses* (New Binary Press, 2017) featured 'Penthouse'; *Counterparts: A Synergy of Law and Literature* (Stinging Fly Press, 2018) featured 'Dignity'; and *The Lonely Crowd* (Issue 13, 2021) published 'Human Soup'.

I would like to thank John Walsh and Lisa Frank of Doire Press for their continued support, professionalism and kindness. Many thanks to Tríona Walsh for the cover design. Heartfelt thanks to the following for their friendship and assistance: Laura McKenna, Fiona Whyte, JP Quinn, Anne O'Leary, Donal Moloney, Deborah Oniah, Mary Morrissy, Arnold J Fanning, Tadhg Coakley and Rachel Andrews. Many thanks also to the following: Kevin Barry, Joseph O'Connor, Carlo Gèbler, John McKenna, Martina Evans, James Harpur, Ciaran Carty, Anthony Glavin, Conal Creedon, William Wall, Liz Kirwan, Nick Kelly, Paul O'Donovan, Claire Connolly, Brian Kirk, Ethel Rohan, Patricia Looney, Ann Luttrell, Gillian Hennessy, Mel Ulm, Colette Sheridan, Jamie O'Connell and Amélia Vincent. Thank you to the School of English at UCC, Triskel Christchurch and Cork City Library. Sincere thanks to the community of readers and writers at Fiction at the Friary, Cork, and a special thank you to my friend and co-founder Danielle McLaughlin.

I am very grateful to the Arts Council of Ireland and Cork City Council for their financial support.

Last but not least, thanks and love to all my family.

MADELEINE D'ARCY was born in Ireland. She spent thirteen years in the UK, where she worked as a criminal legal aid solicitor and as a legal editor in London. She returned to Ireland in 1999 and lives in Cork City with her husband and son.

Madeleine began to write fiction in 2005. In 2010 she received the Hennessy Literary Award for First Fiction and the overall Hennessy Literary Award for New Irish Writer. Her début short story collection, *Waiting for the Bullet* (Doire Press, 2014), won the Edge Hill Readers' Choice Prize 2015 (UK). She holds an MA in Creative Writing (1.1) from University College, Cork, and has been awarded bursaries by the Arts Council of Ireland and Cork City Council. Together with Danielle McLaughlin, she co-hosts Fiction at the Friary, a free monthly fiction event held in Cork City since 2017. She has recently completed a novel.